"Lovers in a dangerous time," to quote lyrics from one of my favorite songs—that's the theme of Emma's Ghost, and the novel develops some poignant and often tragic scenes into a powerful story. I'm not usually big on ghost stories, but this ghost didn't take over the story, but rather was deployed to catalyze a lot of believable drama. Well done, Ms. Karpenko, for your debut novel. What's next?

By PJ Reece, Author

Wonderfully written, this enchanting story melds past and present together with a smooth yet captivating tale. Great read. It is a MUST read.

By Bookworm

A Book that is a Gift

It is such a welcome gift when you find a novel that enchants and excites on so many levels as Emma's Ghost does. This novel delivers all the elements of an intriguing personal mystery, along with a genuine supernatural thriller, while adding a tender love story that spans generations and lifts your spirits as it gently unfolds. -but there is even more for the reader, Emma's Ghost adds genuine 'edge-of-your-seat' suspense by weaving in the true happenings of the historic Halifax Explosion during World War I and the life changing effects it has on the characters as they struggle to cope with the city's utter devastation. Emma's Ghost gives you a front row seat on the action in a page-turner that kept me spellbound from beginning to end. Now, I'm eagerly awaiting Kat Karpenko's next novel. Please, hurry up.

By C.C. Brondwin, author,
Clan of the Goddess, Maiden Magick

Emma is the Glue to Hold Two Interwoven Stories Together

The best aspect of this novel in two parts is hard to pin down. Is it the clever way there are two stories wound into one? The unusual style of telling a partial story for the first half of the book then changing to a chapter per POV (most of the time) to launch a second story, the older history, interspersed with how it matches the (sort-of) present day tale? You'd think it would be daunting, but it's woven together so seamlessly that it's easy to follow.

Is it the history that we get a glimpse of through the eyes of the protagonists? The clear scene-setting that tells of horrific incidents in the most delicate way possible while still honouring the lost and the survivors, and uses details to show the changes in time period clearly for its readers? The awesome cover art? Is it how romance is entangled in a subtle combination with literary fiction, history, mystery, and paranormal themes?

No, the best aspect is Emma. What a character! We feel we know her, even better than Laura. Her moods, her passion, her passive moments, her oneness with the time period--all are masterfully included in this fascinating tale. As would be expected, she is the key to both stories, and her part weaves them together to make one.....

There are mild, non-explicit sexual scenes, implied physical abuse, and emotional abuse portrayed in this book, and all enhance the novel, so I wouldn't have it any other way. But it could be a trigger to some readers. Please know that it's done tastefully with the best of intentions by the novelist....

Bravo to the author for her attention to quality control for the benefit of her readers. Watch for more by Kat Karpenko.
She has natural talent.

By Susan Lauder, Author

Halifax Stars

The star of this beautifully researched romance is the city of Halifax and her citizens' response to the 1917 explosion. Parallel "forbidden" romances in two eras move the narrative along, but the way Karpenko brings history to life was impressive in a first novel, and causes me to eagerly await what treasures she will uncover next.

By Sarah Trevor

Drama with Historical Roots and Heartfelt Passion

With a sudden cold draft and the flash of something red, Laura pulls old letters from a shattered wall. Written from another century, the tenderly loved letters are addressed to a mysterious Emma. Emma's ghost, released to Laura who begins a parallel existence, once was embodied during the time of unimaginable destruction in Halifax Nova Scotia. Laura bravely embarks on a deadly journey to learn the secrets behind the letters and to delve, indeed immerse herself in a war of love and hate that is ageless.

Choosing words to suit the times and the characters, Kat Karpenko has written Emma's Ghost as a love letter to Halifax and her beloved Nova Scotia where heroism and passion abide as they did on December 6th, 1917 when the greatest man-made explosion in pre-atomic time shocked the world. Ms. Karpenko artfully brings this event alive again, connecting up what was viciously divided, while providing a stage for the phantom Emma to shape her anguished destiny. Read on, learn history, enjoy intrigue, feel the love, and let the light of Karpenko's rising star shine for you.

By S.K. Carnes, Author

A Good Read

The story unfolds like opening a time capsule generations later. The devastating tragedies of 1918 in Halifax, Nova Scotia steer the lives of a family in 1985. The characters are strong, smart and beautiful but cannot escape the poignant events of their time. A good read - hard to put down - and written with sensitivity, humor and love for the maritime provinces.

By Marie

A Winner

This was an easy to read, hard to put down romantic story of a modern-day woman's destiny unfolding as she discovers a parallel life of a young woman who lived a century earlier. Plenty of spicy forbidden romance, war time adventure, and the mystery of the supernatural all combined to make this one very nice read. Well done! I will be watching for more.

By Suzanne Van Eislande

Truly enjoyable read. *A love story with a lot of twists and turns. A historical novel providing the reader with an intimate insight of the Halifax explosion. The author gave this reader a lot of emotions to experience.*

By Maureen Stiles

Emma's Ghost

by Kat Karpenko

Emma's Ghost
Copyright © 2017 by Kat Karpenko
All rights reserved.

No part of this book may be reproduced, stored in a retrieval system or transmitted in any form or by any means without prior written permission of the author, except in brief quotations embodied in critical articles or reviews.

Published in Canada by:
Catherine (Kat) Karpenko

katkarpenkoauthor.wordpress.com
authorkkarpenko@gmail.com
facebook.com/authorkatkarpenko

ISBN 978-0-9958934-0-5

*For my loving husband, Gene Hood
whose support has kept me moving forward*

AND

For the memories of the Dear Departed

Table of Contents

Preface i

Acknowledgements iii

PART ONE - THE LETTERS

One - Discovery 3
Two - The Rectory 11
Three - History Project 17
Four - Dream Ghosts 21
Five - Scheming 25
Six - The Work Begins 33
Seven - Charles Lindsay Journals 39
Eight - Not Now 47
Nine - The Key 55
Ten - Party Time 61
Eleven - Fallout 67
Twelve - Stormy Roads 71
Thirteen - Refuge 79
Fourteen - Wounded 83
Fifteen - Restless Night 91
Sixteen - Visitations 97
Seventeen - Rosie Gives Advice 101
Eighteen - A Treasure Is Found 107
Nineteen - The Writing Begins 113

PART TWO - EMMA'S STORY

Twenty - The Meeting *119*
Twenty-One - Hazardous Journey. *125*
Twenty-Two - Mary's Views *131*
Twenty-Three - The Bakers Meet Andrew. *137*
Twenty-Four - Andrew Gets Advice *145*
Twenty-Five - Phone Calls And Messages *149*
Twenty-Six - Emma's Dilemma *153*
Twenty-Seven - Emma's Return *157*
Twenty-Eight - Edgar's Welcome. *161*
Twenty-Nine - Planning The Escape *167*
Thirty - Laura Makes Decisions *171*
Thirty-One - Missing. *179*
Thirty-Two - Conscription. *185*
Thirty-Three - The Orchard *193*
Thirty-Four - Emma's Goodbyes. *197*
Thirty-Five - Recovery *203*
Thirty-Six - The Burgess Farm *209*
Thirty-Seven - News From Town *215*
Thirty-Eight - Edgar's Return *221*
Thirty-Nine - Not Worthy *225*
Forty - A Time For Funerals *229*
Forty-One - Robert's Departure *233*
Forty-Two - Katrina's Birth *239*
Forty-Three - Resolutions. *245*
Forty-Four - Completion *251*

Epilogue *255*

About The Author *259*

Preface

This story was inspired by the discovery of love letters in the wall of a historic house being renovated in Mahone Bay, Nova Scotia. Although I never saw the content of these letters, I thought it was a great plot line for a short story. My Mazatlán writers' group told me different. No. It had the makings of a novel.

The other inspiration was the history that permeates Nova Scotia (where I lived most of my life) and of particular interest, the incredible facts of the 1917 Halifax Explosion that devastated the city during World War I. I have tried to remain true to historical events.

As I persevered, the characters started taking over. Before I knew it, I was transported into two historical time settings, two sets of morality, two dysfunctional marriages, and two emerging love stories born out of chaos and linked by a determined ghost. Perhaps it WAS Emma's ghost that drove me on, just as she obsessed my heroine, Laura.

NOTE: The characters are fictitious, but I have tried to use common names from the south shore of Nova Scotia. Any resemblance to persons living or dead is purely coincidental. I have read the letters (1884-1888) of Ned Harris, a minister of St. James Church, but his character and the rectory he lived in, do not in any way resemble that of Charles Lindsay, the Mahone Bay minister in Emma's story. The Dockside Pub, mentioned in Part One, is also fictitious but has a resemblance to the many fine eateries of Mahone Bay.

Stories and descriptions of the Halifax explosion in Part Two have been based on historical accounts of the time.

Acknowledgements

I would like to thank the members of my Mazatlán Writer's Group who over the years have encouraged me to continue and have shared their knowledge of the craft of writing. The years of input and support from these gifted writers have been extremely instrumental in the development of this work. The following writers have stuck with me to the end (in no particular order): Angela Jackson, Sue Carnes, PJ Reece, Myrna Guymer, Sarah Trevor, Marie Hermanson, Katrine Geneau, Evelyn Wolff. Previous members who have also been most helpful: May Wong, Ken Martens, Mike Latta, Rubye Hinton, David Kindopp, Barbara Horton and our dearly departed fearless leader Rick Azulay.

I must also thank the following for editing assistance: my daughter Sonya Irvine who is a freelance editor, author and friend Lorraine Johnson, and my supportive "readaholic" husband Gene Hood.

Kat Karpenko

- PART ONE -

THE LETTERS

1985
MAHONE BAY, NOVA SCOTIA
CANADA

During a time in history when cell phones and computers were not an integral part of our lives. Personal communications took place with the written word, the telephone, or face to face.

- ONE -

Discovery

Plaster cascaded from the wall filling the air with a fog of fine powder and ancient dust motes. One more swing and Ted broke through the corner of the closet adjoining the exterior wall of the Victorian home. His wife, Laura, insisted that the closet needed to be made larger. A sudden cold draft caused a flutter of something red.

"Wait Ted. There's something behind the laths. It looks like it was hidden in an opening from the closet side." She pointed. "Can you tear that last one off?"

Ted picked up the crow bar and removed it with one muscular tug. Laura coughed through her mask as she reached through the broken corner of the closet to pull out a small bundle covered with dust.

She pulled off her mask. "Wow! These look really old! Who put them here?"

Ted dropped the crow bar and came closer to peer over her shoulder.

With trembling hands, she untied a faded red ribbon wrapped around four letters. Carefully, Laura opened the first pale envelope. The hand-written note on sepia paper, in scratchy black ink, appeared hesitantly scribed, as if written in fits and starts. She read the words to Ted with glowing emphasis.

Lunenburg County
April 3, 1918

My Dearest Emma,

I have spent the week trying to occupy my mind with the daily chores at the acreage. The lambing is near completion and we have kept a watchful eye to keep the coyotes away. The new dogs have worked well and are easy to train.

Even in this busy season I cannot keep you from my thoughts. I am desperate to see you. It feels like an eternity. How can we manage this wait until your husband leaves? Please leave your reply in the usual place.

In the meantime, I will keep the memories of our last sweet embrace in my mind constantly to sustain me.

Your devoted,
Andrew

Laura's large eyes sparked with excitement. She swept her blonde curls away from her face with one hand and clutched the letter to her heart with the other. "Ah, Andrew, you sound divine!"

"Don't be such a drama queen. Divine? Are you kidding? He's screwing with somebody's wife. Not what I would call a prince," Ted exclaimed with indignation.

She stopped and blinked. "Now wait a minute. This was the rectory in the early 1900's, before the new one was built. My God, Ted, I feel like I've opened the proverbial closet full of skeletons. Dare we go on?"

"Laura, could I possibly stop you?" he grimaced, hands on hips.

"Not a mud-wrestling chance, buddy."

Laura put her head to the side and narrowed her eyes. "Who was this Emma? She must be connected to this house. But it was my Gran's house, and her name was Katrina, also known as Kate. My great-grandmother's name was Suzette. No Emmas there. She must have lived here before my great-grandparents. This is going to involve some research. We need some more clues Watson. Let's take a break and read on!"

"But there's still lots more to do. Can't it wait until later?" Ted's voice whined in a weary tone.

She pulled him down next to her on the plaster-covered workbench to examine the contents of the bag more closely.

The letters were in date order, well read, with the corners curled. As she quickly opened the next one, she noticed that they had originally been sealed with wax.

Lunenburg County
April 8, 1918

My Dearest Emma,

I have received your news and grieve daily that we have been parted for such a long time. Edgar's departure cannot come soon enough. It upsets me greatly that your husband would lay a hand on you. To dare such an act in your brother's house is beyond belief. The man is a scoundrel. Drink is no excuse. I highly commend Charles for his actions and wish that I had also been there to protect you.

Having a man of the cloth in the family certainly has some merits. Edgar dare not turn his anger on Charles or the community would react very badly against him. I agree that it is likely true that your brother is torn between his belief in the sanctity of marriage and his desire to have you out of Edgar's grasp, and share your fear that the former may be stronger. You are wise not to tell him of our love until our plans are underway.

My greatest concern is that Edgar will take you away upon his return from sea as he has threatened to do.

Please meet me in the orchard by our favorite tree Sunday evening. We must act soon, my love.

Yours forever,
Andrew

Laura stared up from the letter and cursed under her breath. "That poor woman! What kind of chance was there for her in those days? Divorce was not an option. Women had no rights, not even to their own property." Laura glared angrily. Her voice rose. "Emma was trapped in a brutal marriage!"

"Well, maybe her husband had a right to be upset the way things were going."

"But to physically attack her, Ted! I agree with Andrew. There's no excuse for that. I wonder what happened to her?" She opened the next envelope with little care for the age-worn paper.

Lunenburg County
April 12, 1918

My Dearest Emma,

I think of nothing but our final escape. From dawn to dusk, as I work my way through the endless chores of the farm, the dream of our departure buoys me with happiness.

Every day my mother, Louisa, and I await my brother's return from the war. For her, it is the joy of his presence that brings her happy thoughts. For me, it is the knowledge that he can take over the farm and I will be free. Robert will return soon my love. I ask for your patience although I can hardly bear the burden of time myself.

Very soon, while Edgar is away at sea, you will be able to make your escape. You will be safe here in the country until we can leave for Newfoundland. I know we will find refuge in the coastal village where we will make our new home.

In the meantime, I look forward to our next meeting when our precious moments of bliss will make the waiting less painful.

Your devoted
Andrew

"Wow! The plot thickens!" Laura exclaimed with a playful nudge. "I think there was some hanky-panky taking place in this old town. I wonder if my great-grandparents knew them? I wish Grandmother Kate were still alive so I could ask. But, then, there's Aunt Rosie. She was Gran's friend and might know something. She usually knows all the gossip."

Ted groaned. "Not Aunt Rosie."

Just then an angry blast of cold air whistled through the cracks in the exposed outer walls of the bedroom. Somewhere down the hallway a door slammed violently, rattling the windows. Laura jumped with a start and nervously looked down the hallway. "No one there," she said as she closed the bedroom door.

Ted shivered and grabbed for his sweater.

"You know, we really need to get on with this nasty

job before the snow flies. Besides the oncoming winter, the unchangeable fact is: we're moving in at the end of the month, whether the work is finished or not."

"Oh, I know honey, but there's only one more letter. I can't stop now."

"Okay. Okay. Keep reading. I'll keep on working." Ted muttered testily as he bent over to gather up the bits of plaster and laths for garbage pickup. Laura opened the last envelope and cleared her throat.

Lunenburg County
April 19, 1918

My Dearest Emma,

I am distraught. The letter came today. How can this be happening now? Just as Robert arrived back from the war, the army has decided to conscript me. It is unfair in so many ways. I had no idea that Robert is in such poor condition. He is shattered of mind and body having lost an arm in the war. How can he look after mother and the farm? But she is strong. Somehow things will work out if you can assist her.

Thank you for asking your brother to do something but I cannot shirk my duty. My great-grandparents came here from Germany. They were pioneers. I am proud of them and grateful to the country that took them in, gave them this land. I would not dishonor my family by not serving, or have people think that we side with the Germans.

It is vital that I take you to the farm where you can safely await my return. Edgar will not find you there. Robert and my mother will look out for you, and you can be a great help to them. I pray that the war does not last much longer.

Make ready to leave soon. Please meet me tonight. I cannot wait to hold you in my arms.

Your loving,
Andrew

Laura slowly folded the letter, sighing with furrowed brows. "I have a terrible feeling that this romance did not have a happy ending. Ted, keep ripping those laths. Maybe there are more letters hidden."

Laura rejoined the work pulling at the boards, peering into corners, but the rest of the day's efforts revealed no more secrets.

- two -

The Rectory

Laura felt both relief and apprehension as she finally moved out of their tiny apartment into the house she had inherited, her grandparents' house. She stood on the lawn to admire the work that had been completed to refurbish the outer walls. Originally crafted by a ship builder in 1885 for one of the local captains, the outside featured "gingerbread" woodworking around the roof edge that made it stand out on the street. The ornamental shingles of the roof were crowned with a railed widow's walk that she remembered well. Arched dormer windows extended from both sides of the entrance that had a small roofed porch. Detailed fretwork around the windows and doors were painted brown against the white woodwork of the trim and railings. It was Ted's idea to paint the house teal in contrast, instead of the dull gray it had been as a rectory. She approved of the dramatic effect that resulted.

The former rectory had been left to her mother, May, who could not bear to live there after the tragic automobile accident that took her parents. Besides, May had needed to be near the hospital in Halifax due to the cancer that eventually took her. The house had been rented until recently.

Laura had not lived there since she was a child. That was before her mother's illness, while her father was away with the fishing fleet. So much loss in her life was connected to this place, causing her to resist the idea of moving in, but she remembered how Ted fell in love with it the minute he walked in the door.

"Look at that amazing oak trim around the doorways" he exclaimed running his hand over the circular carving of a sun on the corner.

He gazed up at the lofty ceilings as he walked into the formal dining room. "That sculpted tin ceiling is unique and in pretty good shape for its age. We can make it spectacular, highlight some of the detail in another color when we paint it. That would be a good job for you, honey. You're the artist in the family."

Laura joined in enthusiastically. "And this heavy curved banister! You just don't see this kind of wood or workmanship anymore. It dates to the late 1800's when Nova Scotia was a shipbuilding capital. Men really knew how to work with wood back then. Their homes were their showpieces. This just needs some refinishing to bring back the beauty of the grain."

They followed the banister up to the third-floor attic leading to the widow's walk on top of the house. Ted was not from a sea-faring family, so she had to explain the origin of the name to him.

"This little top deck was traditionally where sailors' wives anxiously searched for the return of their men, often in vain, just like my mother used to do. Unfortunately, the designation proved true to her."

Leaning on the railing, Ted whistled in appreciation as his eyes made a panoramic sweep of the harbor that was the heart of the town named after the bay. Islands could be seen in the distance, just a scattering of the hundreds that nested in this large bay south of Halifax.

Laura was pleased that Ted liked her hometown and wanted to impress him with its history. "Mahone Bay was founded in 1754, one of Nova Scotia's oldest communities. Many of the old houses and warehouses along the shore have been restored and converted to a variety of artisan shops and dining establishments. In the summer, we have a steady stream of tourists stopping in to enjoy the beauty and atmosphere. I guess it's a lot like some of the New England towns."

"Hmmm. That could offer some commercial opportunities for us in the future," Ted mused.

Laura shaded her eyes from the sun with her hand. "I love the history of this place. Can't you just see the three-masted pirate ships anchored out there in the harbor or the privateers pulling into port looking for some sailors to shanghai from the taverns? Those poor lads would sober up on a ship heading for the south seas. Talk about a nasty hangover!"

Her gaze drifted to the islands sheltering the harbor. "There are so many little islands and inlets in the bay for privateers to hide in, it used to drive the English navy mad trying to find them. Mind you, the English navy were not above a bit of kidnapping themselves. Good sailors were highly prized during the age of sail when many lost their lives during a brutally hard existence on the rough seas." Laura's face suddenly clouded over as the loss of her father filled her thoughts.

"Well, Miss History Buff, now it's just a picturesque little tourist haven. The only canons going off are of the camera variety," Ted said stifling a yawn.

Laura's hair flew around her face as the onshore breezes circled. She sighed deeply.

"I remember coming up here with my mother and my grandparents. They let me look through the old telescope and told me to look for Dad's fishing boat on the horizon." The memory was bittersweet.

Ted put his arm around her. "This will be a happy place again, honey. I know you'll do a great job to make it so."

He couldn't wait to begin the interior renovations. As an architect, he was in his glory, constantly taking before-and-after pictures. He was determined to impress the hell out of the senior architects in his firm with the transformation.

Laura was carried away by his flood of ideas and his enthusiasm for turning the old house into their dream home. It almost made her forget the uneasiness she had felt there as a child when she saw the beckoning ghost hiding in dark corners, smiling with mournful eyes. She didn't remember being afraid of the encounters, but it did spook her enough to stay out of the attic. She shook off those silly childhood fantasies. This *WOULD* be their dream home.

Right now, it was a chaotic nightmare, but she didn't have the strength to lift another thing. She undressed in the confusion of the master bedroom letting her clothes fall to the floor without a shred of guilt.

"Honey, where are the towels?" Ted called out from the bathroom.

"You might have thought of that before getting in the shower," she laughed and dug into one of the boxes on the floor.

Tossing him his favorite towel, Laura stopped to admire the auburn curls framing his boyish face, the sculpted muscles of his torso, buttocks and bulging thighs. Someday, when the work on the house was done, she would unearth her art supplies and paint her Adonis in all his glory.

Ted turned and read her gaze. He was not one to miss an opportunity for a romp. Playfully, he took the towel, threw it around her naked back, and pulled her into his damp chest, starting a slow caressing rub with the front of his body. His arousal was immediate.

"I think I would rather use you as my towel" he said in

a deep sexy growl. "Don't you think we need to christen grandma's bed?"

"Okay, lover boy, you talked me into it," she purred back at him enjoying the heat of his searing brown eyes. "Open the wine and I'll slip into the shower."

Perhaps she had a little energy left after all. Happiness spilled from her very pores.

Life is so good right now, it's almost scary. If only it could always be this way.

- THREE -

HISTORY PROJECT

SINCE THEIR MARRIAGE, LAURA HAD ENJOYED WORKING on the house every spare moment. The worst of the work, insulating the outer walls, having the new wallboard installed, and exterior painting was done. Now it was paint and finish time inside. However, she felt lately that she needed something to occupy her mind as well as her body. Her classes were done for her undergraduate degree. Decisions must be made whether to go on for her masters in history, and if so, to choose a topic for her thesis. The small inheritance from her grandparents allowed her the luxury of making this dream come true. Was she up to the challenge?

But ever since finding the letters she could not stop thinking about Emma and Andrew. Who were they? What happened to them? Unravelling the mystery would be her special research project. Perhaps she could incorporate it into her thesis work. That would definitely make it all worthwhile.

She started to plot out her strategies. The town of Mahone Bay is noted for its many churches with their ornately painted steeples. They line the shore of the bay, majestically in a row at the entrance of the town declaring its Christian heritage. She knew her house had been a rectory for St. James Anglican Church. Emma's brother Charles must have been the rector there. She didn't know his last name, but surely there must be records she could search.

Everything would have to wait until the unpacking was finished. By the end of the day, as she worked through organizing their belongings, Laura had formed her plan and could not wait to tell Ted as he came in the door.

He watched with amusement to see her animated face bubbling out words like a cascading brook. Her enthusiasm was child-like. He put on his sternest fatherly voice. "You know whatever makes you happy, makes me happy, BUT don't forget about our main project – THE HOUSE."

"Don't worry honey. I'll have it all under control. I'll be totally yours on the weekends."

Ted peered at her with crescent eyebrows ready to protest.

"I made an appointment with Professor Williams tomorrow," Laura chirped ignoring his look. "If he gives his approval, which I'm sure he will, then the work can begin. I may even get some funding for the research from the historical society. Aunt Rosie will put in a good word for me."

"Oh no, not Aunt Rosie again!" Ted shuddered widening his eyes in mock horror.

"Oh, come on. She's not that bad."

"She's boring. She just repeats her old stories over and over like you've never heard them before. Just don't invite her to dinner, okay? My ears are still recovering from the last gabfest."

A twisted smile flickered across Laura's face. "She's coming on Saturday. Besides, sometimes she drops a little gem of history we haven't heard."

Later, as she tossed sleeplessly in the bed, trying not to wake Ted snoring at her side, her racing thoughts were disturbed by a soft faraway sound. She rose and wrapped a shawl around her thin nightgown, then padded barefoot across the cold wooden floorboards to peer out the window. Nothing was visible but fog reflecting off the streetlights of the harbor road. She never liked the fog, especially at night. It always reminded her of danger - the danger of rocks, unmarked reefs, ships lost. The sound echoed in her ears again, closer this time.

Was that the marker buoy from the harbor moaning its warning? I could swear it was calling my name just now. Funny how sound travels over the water. The buoy is so far away.

Like icy fingers down her spine, a damp chill penetrated the room seeking her out. The hairs on her arms stood up in alert mode, giving her the shivers. She crept silently back to the bed in the total darkness and pulled the down-filled covers to her ears like a cocoon. Sleep did not come easily, nor did it provide the rest she was seeking, only an eerie disturbing dream.

- FOUR -

DREAM GHOSTS

ON THE ROOF, AT THE RAIL OF THE WIDOW'S WALK, A FIVE-year-old child in a frilly pink dress and matching silk shoes was trying to hold up the telescope and squint with one eye. She was searching the harbor.

"I can't see it. Where do I look?"

A shadowed woman with a young face and ancient eyes took her hand. She wore an old-fashioned, ankle-length skirt touching laced, pointed boots. A long-sleeved, white blouse buttoned closely to her throat was adorned with an elaborate embroidered collar that circled her long slender neck. Her narrow waist was cinched with a red velvet ribbon matching the one around her cascading raven curls. As the woman's face shone in the sunlight, the child was captured by her radiant beauty, and inhaled the sweet scent of lavender that surrounded them in a cloud.

"Hold it up and look to the right, my dear. Don't look to the harbor. There now, see the road going down the hill. See the brown and white steeple and the house beside it. You will find the answers there."

"But I was looking for father's boat. What am I looking for?"

The woman's voice turned into an eerie tremor. *"Seek and ye shall find the true past, present, and future. I can guide the way."*

"But where am I going?"

When she heard no answer, the child put down the telescope and turned to look for the woman. The widow's walk was deserted.

"Where are you? Where did you go?" She ran down the steps into the attic looking around the room lit only by light coming from one small window.

"Are you playing hide and seek?"

Suddenly a figure dressed in white gauze floated out of a dark corner. Long silvery hands reached out to tenderly touch her blonde ringlets. The child looked up into the hooded face and beamed.

"Mommy, it's you! I thought I lost you Mommy. Where did the lady go?" She reached out with eager arms.

The white figure enveloped the child in a misty blanket of love. "Listen to your Grandma, Laura. I love you. I will always be near you," she whispered softly.

"Was that Gran, Mommy? She didn't look like my Gran. Why was she here?"

"Yes, this other grandmother has come to help you. I can say no more. Only she can show you the path."

The white figure turned and vanished into the darkness like a wisp of smoke. Laura ran after her crying.

"Mommy, don't go! I need you. Don't go!" Her tears flowed freely from a bottomless sorrow deep inside.

Ted woke up with a start. "Laura, Laura wake up." He grabbed her sobbing, twitching body and shook her. "You're having a bad dream. It's one of your damn nightmares."

Laura's bleary eyes opened and she tried to focus, choking back sobs, still feeling the vice-like pain in her chest. Words exploded from her as she grabbed onto her husband.

"Oh Ted, it was so real this time. I was a little girl and my mother was in the attic and there was a woman. She told me I needed to find something so I could find my way and my mother said it was my Gran but I didn't recognize her. She appeared so young, so different!" Laura gasped for air.

"Take it easy. It was just a dream. Coming back to this house has stirred up a lot of painful memories. Close your eyes and try to let them go. Let's try to get back to sleep. Tomorrow's a busy day," Ted said wearily, stifling a yawn. He put his arm around her shoulders drawing her into the warmth of his body. The comforting heat slowly brought her back from the darkness.

He's right. It was just another one of my nightmares where I'm talking to my mother and suddenly she's gone. We were in this house together so often. The memories got hold of me. But it was all so real this time!

As she drifted in a sea of semi-consciousness outside of the deep sleep she sought, the strange grandmother's words circled the walls of her mind.

Seek and ye shall find the true past, present, and future. I can guide the way.

- FIVE -

SCHEMING

LAURA CHECKED HERSELF IN THE ELEVATOR MIRROR. She felt a wreck after the fretful sleep last night, but had done her best to hide the dark circles under her eyes. She took special care to arrange her hair in a sophisticated up-do, with curls pulled away from her face, and rippling down her back in silky, sun-streaked rivulets. Even though she did not need them at the moment, the reading glasses perched on her nose, gave her, what she perceived to be, an intellectual look. The emerald sweater with a deep v-neckline was her favorite, bringing out the green and gold of her hazel eyes. Her short skirt revealed athletic, shapely legs.

She remembered hearing an attractive younger classmate talking about Professor Williams. "It's a shame about his wife dying so young. He always looks a little sad, but he's SO good-looking. Although he checks out the ladies, it's strictly look and don't touch. I get no vibes from him at all."

However, as Laura patted her hair into place, she thought putting on her best appearance should help the cause. When dealing with men, this had always been successful. "If my outfit doesn't grab his attention, I would suggest he have his eyes checked."

She got out at the history department of the Dalhousie University Arts Centre and knocked on an office door inscribed with the name Dr. Raymond Williams, Postgraduate Studies.

"Ah, Laura, come in. Nice to see you." He flashed a blazing smile and gestured for her to take a seat across from him. "I assume you're here to talk about taking your Master's degree." He removed his glasses and tucked them in the breast pocket of his sports jacket.

Sitting down on a rather low slung chair Laura was forced to look up at the aristocratic features of a surprisingly young-looking face, complemented by a thick crown of salt-and-pepper hair swept over one eyebrow. She noticed that his gaze was not focused on her eyes as she began to speak but glanced off the emerald green of her sweater. He leaned forward, hands folded on the desk, in a pose of concentration.

"Yes, professor. I'm going to take the plunge and have a topic I want to pursue. As you've been my mentor during my prep courses, I thought I'd run it by you before making a formal proposal. I'd also be extremely pleased if you could find the time to be my thesis advisor."

She could see him visibly puff up with the flattery as he casually leaned back in his chair. The face turned benevolent, the voice encouraging. "I'd be happy to look over your proposal, Laura. What topics appeal to you?"

"I've always been interested in Nova Scotia history in the period of the First World War. I've been thinking how devastating it must have been for a small town like Mahone Bay to deal with conscription, agricultural demands of the war effort, and the devastation of the 1917 Halifax explosion. On top of everything else, the Spanish flu epidemic had hit the countryside. Since the loss of life was significant, the surrounding farm community must have been badly affected by the lack of manpower. How did they cope with it all? I want to focus on the impact the war had on Nova Scotia rural communities using Mahone Bay as a model. I grew up there and know there is a lot of archival material available in the local museum." She paused to take a breath.

Williams smiled broadly. "Well, Laura, I see you've put some thought into this. Interesting. Write up your proposal and I'll submit it to the academic committee. I know your marks are high enough to proceed. You have a good background in history and sociology. We can work out the details together later. I would be glad to be your thesis advisor."

"Thank you Professor. I'll have it to you this week."

Laura hummed to herself as she descended in the elevator thinking, "One very male professor down, one sweet old lady to go."

Back home the next day, Laura looked out the window to

see a bent-over figure making her way up the walkway with the use of a cane. Her hand-knit, red tam was slightly askew, partially covering the long silver braid that hung down her back. She couldn't help thinking that it seemed like only yesterday when her aunt was tall and agile, always up for a game, or a long walk in the woods. She loved those camping trips when Rosie and Gran took her to Kedji, that beautiful national park in the center of the province. The clear, tea-colored lakes and rivers of the Mi'kmaq native hunting grounds were still surrounded by towering, unspoiled forests. Those two dear ladies taught her to love the natural beauty of the province.

Her memories were interrupted by a knock on the door. "She's here, Ted. Now promise me you'll be nice. She's just a lonely old gal with a heart of gold."

"I will be my ever-charming, polite, sweet-talking self." He posed briefly with a false smile, then added, "But I can't promise I won't doze off during the second hour."

"Uh-huh. Perhaps you should have coffee instead of wine."

"Oh, no! Wine is absolutely essential under the circumstances."

"Well don't forget to ply Aunt Rosie with wine as well and she likes a wee drop of cherry brandy too."

Laura opened the large oak door of the main entrance making a mental note that it needed to be refinished when they were doing the banisters. The ornate carving of intertwining leaves around its window would be tricky.

"Aunt Rosie, how nice to see you!" Laura put her arms around the fragile frame of the stooping figure, gave her a gentle hug, and a kiss on the cheek.

"Just grand ta see ya, my lovely. I'm tickled pink ya've both decided ta settle here instead of Halifax." She straightened to receive Ted's brisk hug. "Ted, ya handsome devil, yer goin' ta have yer hands full restorin' this old place. But it's got so much style and history. I've always loved it and bein' here brings back so many grand memories of Kate and that rascal husband of hers. Did I ever tell ya about the time we went ta the church picnic?"

"Yes, I think I remember that story, Aunt Rosie. Let me take your coat and hat. Come sit down in the living room and I'll get you a nice glass of cherry brandy."

"Ah, yes, thank ya, Ted. That would be lovely." Aunt Rosie made her way slowly into the room off the entranceway using her cane and sat in one of the chintz-covered overstuffed chairs. She sighed a little as she edged back against the high back of the chair and reached for the brandy Ted handed her. "Ah, that's some good," she murmured with pleasure.

"Ya know I'm still recuperatin' from that hip operation last summer. Took all the good outta me fer a spell. Now with winter comin' on, the cold doesn't help these ol' joints. I don't seem ta have the stamina for standin' too much either." She blinked several times. Her grey-blue eyes stared blankly ahead. "Now, where was I?"

"Aunt Rosie, before you continue with your story I've

some exciting news to tell you. I've decided to continue with my studies to do a master's degree in history. I'm going to do it about the effects of the First World War on Mahone Bay and similar rural communities. It'll mean I can base a lot of my research here."

"Why, that's wonderful, dear. Your Grandma Kate would be so proud. Ya know she was a bit of a student of history too. Not in an academic sense, but she was interested in the history of the area. We both were. She helped establish the Historical Society and the local museum, ya know. She's responsible fer a lot of things we now have in the archives. We used ta go out ta estate sales ta beg and barter."

"Yes, I do know, Aunt Rosie, and I also know that you are still an active member. I was wondering if I could ask you to put in a good word for my project. I would be glad to donate the finished work to the museum."

"I'm sure they'll be pleased as punch ta assist in any way. In fact, there may be some money available ta help with yer research. We get a little grant every year. I'll talk to Edna, the secretary, tomorrow."

"You're a peach. I knew I could count on you." Laura bent over to give her a squeeze.

"Easy, young lady. These bones are brittle." Rosie smiled her crooked smile, her eyes twinkling.

"Okay, ladies, now that the business part of the evening is over, can we please eat?"

"Charming, Ted, very charming," Laura said, adding

a playful slap to his shoulder as she moved towards the dining room table.

"Well, you did put together a damn fine dinner. I've been smelling this roast lamb for hours, and to help celebrate, we have a nice cabernet in your honor, Aunt Rosie. May I escort you to the dining room?" he asked, taking her hand to help her out of the chair.

"Thank you, dear boy. I've so much ta tell ya about this house."

Laura stopped with ears tuned in to hear the talk.

"Did ya know it was originally built fer a sea captain? But then, he fell on hard times, and had ta sell it ta the church. Then, Reverend Lindsay and his family lived here. I used ta visit his wife at the nursing home. Such a lovely lady. His brother-in-law was a scoundrel, though. I heard tell he used ta go rum running, and drank more than his share." She paused with a question puzzling her face. "Don't know what happened ta his wife though. She just up and disappeared. Some says he took her off ta the south seas. Others say they can still see her walkin' the widow's walk."

"Now that's interesting." Laura muttered to herself, but didn't want to interrupt as Rosie rambled on.

"Now the Lindsays were related ta my uncle Bertram's wife, Bessie. There was a character! Crazy as a bag of hammers! She had no truck with the church, no how; had twelve children, and gave them all devils' names. I can still see her standing at the back-kitchen door callin' out their names ta come fer supper. All the Catholics would be crossin' themselves." Rosie boomed her sonic belly laugh, wiping at her eyes.

"Yes, we sure have our share of characters in the family. Old Mephistopheles lives up by the graveyard. Course everyone calls him Meppy. His sons Peter and Matthew still live here, as well as his daughter Ann. He didn't want ta keep up his mother's tradition with the names," she chuckled.

Ted pulled out a chair from the large oak table. "Sit here at the head of the table, Aunt Rosie."

"Thank you dear." She adjusted the glasses that slid down her nose and stared blankly into a void. "Now, where was I?"

Standing behind Rosie, Ted rolled his eyes upwards. Laura turned into the kitchen with a grin to get dinner on the table. She made a mental note to have a detailed conversation with Aunt Rosie about the Lindsays and the lady viewed on the widow's walk.

- SIX -

The Work Begins

Laura examined the impressive church steeple piercing the heavens like the spearhead of God. She wondered how anyone was able to paint the lofty vertical sides contrasting the soft yellow with the rich brown turning to red on the steeple. It was obviously a labor of love.

A voice startled her from behind. "It's beautiful, isn't it?"

She turned to see a middle-aged, balding man coming up the walkway carrying a bouquet of lilies. A closer look revealed a starched white collar.

"Amazing. I've admired this church since I was a child. My name is Laura McGinty. Are you the minister here?"

"Yes, Darcy Hennigar, at yer service," he replied in the soft south shore accent so familiar to her. "Glad ta meet ya Ms. McGinty. I don't recall seeing ya here before."

"My husband and I just moved to Mahone Bay. We're living in my grandparents' house. Katrina and James Martin were their names, also known as Kate and Jim.

"Oh, yes, they lived in our former rectory. Such a wonderful old place."

"My husband is an architect and he's taking it on as a restoration project."

"That's wonderful news. It's so much a part of this town. Just splendid! I must let our parishioners know. Would ya care to look inside the church?"

"Thank you. I would." Laura followed him through the heavy wooden door and stopped inside to stare at the stained-glass windows framed by Gothic arches. Carefully crafted pews flanked a red carpet leading to an altar. On the walls, religious carvings, dating back to the days of ship building and expert woodworking, completed the serenity of the interior.

Without warning, the slightly musty smell of long-used prayer books, mixed with the fumes of extinguished candles, and the strong fragrance of the lilies, transported her to another time, and another church. The numbness of grief thawed, unleashing a flood of pain. She grasped the back of a pew to steady herself.

Reverend Hennigar placed the flowers on the altar and turned to see a tear sliding down Laura's cheek. "Are ya all right Missus McGinty?"

Laura swallowed hard and spoke slowly. "It's just that the last time I was in a church it was my mother's funeral. That was only a year after my grandparents were killed."

Reverend Hennigar's eyes softened and he took her hand. "My condolences. Ya must have been close ta them. I remember reading about the highway accident that took yer grandparents at the Lunenburg crossroads, but I didn't know yer mother died as well. That's an awful bad loss fer ya all at once."

"Yes, cancer took her very quickly. I had just started university when she was diagnosed, then I decided to take a few years off to look after her. It was just Mom and me for many years. Dad was lost at sea when I was ten. It's hard to accept that all my family are now gone."

"Not gone, my dear, not forgotten. As long as you're alive, their spirits will live in yer heart. In God's kingdom, all good people shall be united." He observed her earnestly with eyebrows raised. "Do ya have faith, Missus McGinty?"

Laura appeared confused, and awkwardly withdrew her hand. "It's hard to believe in a kindly God when He takes your loved ones."

Reverend Hennigar raised his bushy eyebrows, this time in protest, and was about to speak when Laura cleared her throat, and quickly went on.

"I guess I've digressed from the real reason for my visit. It involves a research project I'm doing for my master's degree. I was wondering if you have any historical information, birth and death records around the time of the First World War. I'm doing a study on the effects of the war on small towns such as Mahone Bay. My Aunt Rosie thought there might be some old diaries that were kept by the churchmen of that time."

"Rosie Langille? Is she yer aunt?"

"Yes, that's her, but she's not really my aunt. I have

always called her Aunt Rosie. She was a close friend of my grandmother Kate."

"She's quite a source of information, yer Aunt Rosie. I don't think there's anythin' goin' on round here that Rosie Langille doesn't know about. Of course, she's right about the diaries. There was one rector that had extensive diaries; I do believe they covered that period. I can dig them out for ya if ya like. We have many historical items stored away where the salt air can't get at 'em."

"Reverend Hennigar, that would be wonderful! When could they be available?"

"Well, first of all, if we're going ta be friends, ya'll have ta start calling me Darcy like everyone else. Just leave me yer phone number and I'll give ya a call when we've dusted them off. And lastly, if ya ever need a friendly ear ta tell yer problems to, I'm available. "No preachin'. I promise," he added with a wink.

"Well, then, I 'll have to be Laura to you. Thanks, Darcy."

Laura returned home charging up the steps two at a time, eager to tell Ted the good news. "Honey, I've just met the nicest ..." One look at the fire in Ted's eyes stopped her in mid- sentence. "What's wrong?"

"You were supposed to be here to let the workmen in so they could redo the fireplace." His scowl changed her sunshine into clouds.

"I'm sorry. I thought you said they were coming tomorrow."

"For God's sake, write it down, Laura. You know you can't keep track of things unless you write them down. They called me at work when I was in a very important meeting. If I'm going to make partner in this firm, I have to look professional. I can't be running off in the middle of the day. I'm counting on you to be on top of things. Your little research project isn't going to pay the bills."

The words cut deep. Her *little* research project meant a lot to her. "Sorry Ted, I'll try to do better. I'll get supper on." She turned her back and muttered to herself. "He didn't even notice that I finished painting the dining room walls yesterday. I took the morning off to take a jog along the river. So, shoot me." She stomped towards the kitchen walking around the debris left at the fireplace by the workers. "Guess I'll have this mess to clean up too!"

The little pain she was feeling in her temples suddenly loomed large. Ted's anger enflamed her own, but it wasn't worth the fight it would cause, his hurtful words that could never be unsaid. She wasn't feeling strong enough to bear the fallout of his tantrums right now. It was difficult at the best of times. His bad moods were getting more frequent, but they were usually short-lived. He would feel better after supper. Maybe, after the renovations were over, the old Ted would return to her.

The jangle of the phone pierced her dark thoughts. "Hello Laura. It's Darcy. I just wanted ta tell ya that I found the diaries of Charles Lindsay and they are from

1910 to 1918.

"Perfect. I'll be by tomorrow to have a look. Thanks, Darcy."

Laura put the phone down slowly. The realization struck her like a blow to the forehead. As she put the pieces together, her excitement rose.

Charles Lindsay was the rector here at the time of the letters! It fits - Emma's brother's name was Charles! Aunt Rosie was talking about the Lindsays. She knew his wife. She's bound to have more clues. But who was Andrew? How could she find out about him? There was much more mystery to sort out.

- SEVEN -

CHARLES LINDSAY JOURNALS

Laura walked to the church hall with her hands buried in her pockets. The gentle autumn had turned cruel. A nor'easter was churning off the coast bringing icy winds to rob the trees of their remaining foliage. The worst of the season was coming, and she was already missing the warmth of the sun. The dampness seeped into her bones spreading an aching fatigue.

Darcy's smiling face greeted her at the door. "Nice ta see ya, Laura. Come on in out of the cold, girl, right quick."

He showed her through the hall into his office where several stacks of journals were piled on top of the file cabinet. Bookshelves with rows of scholarly books surrounded the room. Laura sensed that this was his sanctuary. He was at home behind his antique roll-top desk, perched on a rotating chair. Looking like a beneficent leprechaun, he had the gift of putting her at ease, as if they had known each other for a long time.

He gestured emphatically with his short arms as he spoke. "I thought ya could take the Lindsay journals into our workshop which usually isn't used durin' the day. You're goin' ta have fun sortin' through all this stuff. His penmanship isn't too bad though. I tried lookin' at a few volumes, but got lost and a little bored with all the details."

"That's all right Darcy. Details are what I'm interested in. Also, would you have any church records for the early 1900's for births, marriages and deaths?"

"Sure enough, what exactly are ya lookin' for?"

"Would it be possible to verify that Emma Lindsay was Charles Lindsay's sister? I am curious to see what happened to her. I think she was married to a man named Edgar around 1916. It would be very useful to know their last name."

"I'll have a look, but the records may be in Halifax, if they were married there. On the other hand, many records were destroyed during the Halifax Explosion of 1917. I'll call some of my contacts in the city ta check fer ya. Since Charles Lindsay was originally from Prince Edward Island, I may not have a birth record fer his sister. If she was livin' at the rectory, though, Rosie Langille might know of her. She used ta visit old Mrs. Lindsay, Charles's wife, at the nursin' home. They used ta swap stories fer hours until poor Mrs. Lindsay got dementia."

"I was thinking Aunt Rosie would be a good source. I'm getting together with her soon."

"Yes, she's like a livin' encyclopedia of the town, our

Rosie. But watch out. Once you've opened a volume there's no tellin' where ya'll end up, or how long it'll take." Darcy warned with a grin and a wink.

Laura nodded and smiled as she thought of her dinner with Rosie. "Oh, I do understand Darcy. Thanks for the heads up."

She shuffled through her notebook, hesitated, then decided to go for it. "Now the other person I was trying to research is a man called Andrew from the Lunenburg area who was conscripted into the army in 1918. He was a farmer."

Darcy furrowed his brow. "I think yer best bet would be the Nova Scotia Archives. Ya may be able ta get conscription lists from that time fer Lunenburg County."

"Looks like I'll have to make a trip to Halifax soon. Besides, I need to meet with my thesis supervisor. In the meantime, I'll be looking at these journals. Thanks so much for your help, Darcy."

"Let me know if there's anythin' else ya need. I'm here most days, and when I'm not, Angus, our caretaker can let ya in."

Laura spent the rest of the day reading. The hours slipped by as she found herself immersed in the busy life of a parish cleric at the turn of the twentieth century. All the while her mind wandered to thoughts of Emma and Andrew, seeking clues about how their lives evolved. The mystery lingered, drawing her further and further into frustration, as if their lives and hers were part of a novel she was reading that had no ending.

Hearing Darcy getting ready to leave, Laura glanced at her watch, and could not believe it was six o'clock. Ted would be home already. She scrambled to get her notes together and met up with Darcy at the door.

"Sorry, I sort of lost track of time."

"No problem, Laura. It's nice havin' ya round. Hope you're findin' the diaries useful."

"Yes, they're giving a face to the village at the time. It was a beehive of activity with the shipbuilding, the fishery, and the new railway connections. The war effort must have doubled the work load for most people. This is an area with many German settlers. I wonder how they felt about the war, and whether they were treated any differently because of it."

"Well, knowin' folks as I do, I'd say there might've been some harsh words spoken against the German settlers even though some of them originally settled here way back in 1754. People like the Ernsts and the Zwickers built this town. In those times, German settlers and their businesses likely worked twice as hard as anyone else ta keep things goin'. But war brings out the worst in people and there's always bitterness accompanyin' loss."

"So right. Labeling people as enemies, just because of their ethnic background, never seemed fair to me." Laura threw on her coat, and rushed through the door that Darcy held open. "Sorry I've got to dash. There's no supper ready for my hubby. See you soon. Thanks again."

Laura rushed up the walkway pushing against the bitterness of the wind. Just as she had feared, glaring from the front window, Ted's handsome features turned sour when she approached. He stood in the entranceway, hands on hips, his eyes as dark and stormy as a hurricane sea. His greeting was just as cold.

"Where the hell have you been? I've been home for over an hour."

As she brushed by him, apprehension swelled inside her. His breath was heavy with the smell of rum. "Sorry Ted. I've started reading the journals of Charles Lindsay who was the rector here during the First World War, and I just lost track of time. Remember, I told you that I was going to the church to do research this morning."

Ted followed her in heavy-footed strides. "That was this morning and now it's well past supper time. You need to manage your time better, Laura. Being late is becoming an annoying habit of yours."

She turned to face him. "Try to think of it as a job, Ted. This is what I'll be doing for the next two years."

"Well what about the job I'm doing. You know, the one that brings home the bacon. You haven't devoted much time to the renovation project lately. I need to have it completed by the summer and you know how tight the budget is. You've got to be a part of this."

Laura swallowed hard, reining in her emotions. "I know, honey. I can handle it all. I'm going to get work done this weekend. I'll go into Halifax with you tomorrow to get some special paint for the dining room ceiling. I'll see about getting some scaffolding too, then drop in on Professor Williams to discuss my thesis work."

Ted's eyes rolled upwards. "What sexy little outfit are you going to wear this time?"

"What are you talking about?"

"I see how you dress when you meet with him. You may get more supervision than you bargained for."

Her voice rose as she emphasized every word. "You are being ridiculous!"

"Not as ridiculous as you, if you think flirting is going to get you a master's degree. It'll more likely result in a mistress degree."

Laura's eyes fired through him like flaming spears. She stomped out of the room, trembling with anger. "I can't talk to you when you're like this."

"That's right, Laura run away and hide. I'll just go down to the pub for my supper," he shouted, slamming the door behind him.

These fits of jealousy had always been the most difficult part of their relationship. This time, she could not get past her own anger to smooth it over. Always being on the defensive was wearing her down.

Why was he always raining on her parade? She had never been unfaithful to him. Why was he always accusing her?

As she climbed the stairs to their bedroom, the tears began to flow. There was no stopping the salty sting of them. The quilted covers of her grandmother's bed formed a refuge as she curled her knees to her chin. In this womb of safety, she allowed the floodgate to open. Anger, pain, sadness, and grief tumbled out of the dark places. Eventually, tears gave way to a weighty weariness.

On the doorstep of dreams, she thought she heard the sweet refrain of a soothing Celtic lullaby singing softly through her mind like the breath of angels. A warm, tender hand brushed the cares from her forehead. The sweet voice whispered.

Rest now, Laura. Blessed are the sleeping, for they can feel no pain.

- EIGHT -

NOT NOW

LAURA SLEPT LATE THE NEXT MORNING WAKING WITH A dull, groggy head, unwilling to accept the daylight. Through bleary eyes she realized Ted had already left for work. The car keys were on the table with a note.

Got a ride with Bill. Working late. Call when you get home.

Were the keys a peace offering or was he still mad? Not a particularly warm and fuzzy note. Guess she would find out when he got home. His temper was like fireworks. It went off with a bang then fizzled out after he had his rant. Unfortunately, it always left her rattled and uncertain of what came next. Her upbringing had not prepared her. She could not remember angry words being spoken by her parents or grandparents. She did not inherit any tools to deal with his outbursts.

If he had shown her this side of him before they were married, her life might be different now. He had pursued her with loving kindness when she was lonely and vulnerable after the deaths in her family. All her university friends had moved away to find work and were busy raising families.

Did she ignore the negative side of his personality because of her need?

Of course she did!

The warning signs had been there: the unreasonable jealousy, the out-of-control temper, the periodic binge drinking. At first, his constant watch over the attentions of other men was flattering. Then, there was the night of the bar fight when a former boyfriend came too close. The ensuing bloody brawl was scary and embarrassing. Later, his anger mixed with jealousy. He cursed and blamed her because she was flirting. Yet, she knew she never gave him just cause to doubt her fidelity. Foolishly, she appeased him with sex thinking it would prove her love. The make-up sex was always good. Pleasing her sexually was his way of showing her he was sorry...until the next time.

A busy day was before her. No time to worry about Ted now. She would use a little sugar to smooth it all over, like icing an imperfect cake. Appeasement was the only tool known to her, but it never resolved the problems.

One problem at a time became her mantra. Call Professor Williams to see when he would be available. What to wear? Ted's words seared through her memory. Maybe he was right about her apparel. She shrugged and chose her favorite jeans with a blue sweater that clung softly to her curves. A pair of knee-length boots completed the casual-chic persona she wanted for the day.

After dashing around town doing errands she felt exhausted, but before meeting with the prof she put on a cheery face. "Professor Williams I'm so glad you were available this afternoon."

"Always have time for my favorite student. Have a seat Laura and please call me Ray like the rest of my cohorts."

"Well, I had no idea I had reached the cohort status."

He gave her one of his disarming smiles, then looked at her intently. "You have the brains and the ability to go far in the academic world. I'm more than happy to be associated with your project. I have a special fondness for Mahone Bay and have a good collection of history books on the South Shore. I think we'll make a good team."

Laura cleared her throat, caught a little off guard by the compliment. The recognition felt especially good right now. She returned his smile. "Thank you, Ray. I think so too."

The next two hours passed quickly as Laura talked excitedly about the Lindsay diaries and the picture she was forming of the time. She took notes on recommendations for future research, got the name of the best person to contact at the archives, and left the office with an invitation to look through his library for other references.

Her hurried trip to the Nova Scotia Archives produced the information she wanted most - Andrew's last name. Andreas Burgess was conscripted in Lunenburg County in April of 1918. Bingo! It was the only name close to Andrew. The date fit and he was of German descent. He would have changed the name to Andrew in Nova Scotia in order to fit in. It was common practice among immigrants, especially their children, to adopt anglicized names.

Ideas buzzed through her brain like hornets as she sat in the rush hour traffic. This information was going to seriously distract her from her thesis research. Yet something in her psyche yearned to know more. The importance of knowing what happened to Andrew and Emma was like a weed taking hold, growing out of control. She was sure she was on the right track.

The clock in the foyer was chiming seven as she climbed the stairs of the front porch hauling paint cans. When she opened the front door, the blinking light of the answering machine gave her an uneasy feeling.

Ted's voice sounded tired and irritable. "Laura I'm heading to the Dockside Pub. Meet me there for supper when you get in. I've got something important I want to talk to you about." The message was sent at six.

Her stomach tightened. He would be well into the rum by now. She turned a weary look into the hallway mirror, ran a brush through her disheveled curls and outlined her lips in a vibrant red to distract from the tired lines around her eyes.

She did like the historic old pub with its creaky floorboards dented by salty storytellers' boots, its wood marinated by rum, beer, sea salt, and time. In rum running days, the building was a warehouse where the precious cargo was stored before putting off to American ports. Prohibition was good for Mahone Bay. Fortunes were made by merchants and fishing captains alike. Rumors existed regarding the tradition of stills in the back woods being very much alive today.

A modern entrepreneur thought the old building was a perfect place for a pub and filled it full of mariner's treasures, from ship's bells to ancient sea charts. Round windows overlooked the bay. In the summer months, the outside deck was an appealing location to breathe in the fresh Atlantic breezes while sipping on a tasty, local brew. The food was good and plentiful. It was soon a popular tourist destination. At this time of year, the pub was less crowded relying on the local trade, the after work assortment of professionals, tradesmen, and casual diners.

Laura spotted Ted at the bar engrossed in conversation with an attractive, blonde bar maid in tight jeans and pub T-shirt. He turned, half smiling at Laura in a rosy glow. "Hi honey. You're back from the big city. Get everything done? Meet Cindy. This lovely, young lady has been taking good care of me."

"I can see that. Hi Cindy."

"How's it goin'. What can I get ya Missus McGinty?"

"A Keith's draught sounds good, thanks." She turned to Ted and tried to read his mood. "Let's get a table. Have you eaten?"

"No, I was waiting for you, honey. It's been a long

time since we had a night out. We need to spend more time together." They found a table near the front window.

Ted's speech had a familiar slur and his gaze was intense as he grasped her hand.

"Laura I've been thinkin'. Could you put your research project off for a couple of years? I really need you on my side right now and hell, it's about time we started a family. You're turnin' thirty soon. The clock is tickin'."

She was unable to respond, her mind searching for some meaning.

Where was this coming from? They had agreed that she would complete her degree now, and wait before starting a family!

"Well, how about it?"

"Ted you know I want to have kids at some point, but I don't think this is the time or the place to discuss this. It's not something I can decide on the spur of the moment. You're asking me to give up a lot. Why now?"

"Do you have to go consult the prof? Get his permission?" Ted's voice boomed. A couple at the neighboring table turned to look at him. He didn't notice. Laura did. Her face flushed with embarrassment.

"No way," she hissed. "I make my own decisions, and this is a big one. I'm tired. Let's talk about it at home."

"You're just going to put it off, just like you're putting off all my plans."

More eyes were turning their way.

"You go home and think about it. I'm going to stay for

another drink."

There was no reasoning with him in this state. She left her untouched beer on the table.

"Don't wait up for me," echoed off the walls as she walked out the door.

Sleep did not come easily that night as Laura fought between her anger and her desire to preserve her marriage. He was being unreasonable to ask this of her now. Why was it so important to him? Was she able to make this sacrifice? No solutions surfaced as she tossed from side to side. The clock showed it was past midnight and Ted had not returned. Speculating where he might be only made her angrier.

Desperate for sleep, she decided to go downstairs for some warm milk. A cool breeze greeted her at the bedroom door. The hairs on her arms suddenly stood up in prickly alarm. The scent of lavender filled her nostrils, choking her senses.

Hovering at the top of the stairs a white, wispy light appeared. From its center the form of a woman dressed in black mourning clothes grew from child to adult-size and reached towards her.

The woman in my dream on the widow's walk! The woman Mom said was my other Gran! Was her foggy brain playing tricks on her?

The sad, beautiful eyes clearly spoke to her without sound.

Not now, Laura. Not now!

Behind Laura's eyes, lights suddenly spun in circles like a revolving top. Her balance wavered. A heavy curtain of darkness descended on her, ending with a thud, as her limp body hit the floor.

- NINE -

THE KEY

ANGRY THUMPING CHALLENGED LAURA'S EYELIDS TO open. She raised her head trying to focus, her thoughts spinning. She was in the darkened hallway.

What happened? Why was she on the floor?
THE GHOST!
The woman on the stairs was the woman in her dream! How is it possible?

The banging continued, now with an accompanying bellow. It was not in her head. It was at the front door.

"Laura are ya there? For Christ's sake open up. I don't have my keys."

Ted's growly voice hacked at her confusion like a machete. Pain got in the way of her every movement. "I'm coming, Ted. Give me a minute," she shouted as loud as she could.

Hoping to calm the impending tantrum, she rose painfully to her feet, pushing off the hard wooden floorboards. There would be bruises for certain. Gripping the banister of the curved staircase, she made it down to the entranceway to unlock the heavy oak door, and stood clinging to the handle.

Ted bulldozed into the entranceway nearly knocking her over. "What the fuck took you so long. My house key was with the car...." Ted stopped, noticing Laura's pale face and slightly swollen cheek. Her nightdress clung to her body with the hem twisted to one side. He took an unsteady step towards her trying to focus on her face.

"What the fuck happened? You're a mess."

Leaning on the door to steady herself, she raised her hand to her forehead, and expelled the words in one breath. "I saw the ghost of the woman in my dreams; then woke up on the floor."

"That's crazy. Are ya sure ya didn't have a fall, banged yer head, and THEN imagined the dream ghost?"

"I'm sure Ted. Positive. I know what I saw…or else…I may be losing it. It's like this woman is haunting me. It's unreal. I can't figure out why."

"Well that's what I've bin trying ta tell ya," he slurred. "Yer walkin' round in a daze most o' the time tryin' ta juggle too many balls. Ya gotta focus on what's important. Ya gotta give up yer school work and this obsession with the letters."

"Let's not get into it again," she sighed. "I just need some rest. It'll make more sense in the morning."

"Okay. Not now. But we're goin' ta have this conversation again."

Ted gripped the banister, and put a muscular arm around Laura as they leaned on each other, moving slowly up the stairs. He helped her onto the bed, watched her sink into the pillow, and immediately disappear into deep sleep.

"I don't know what's gotten inta her lately," he muttered as he undressed in front of the closet mirror. He glanced up to see a puffy red face with new lines forming around the eyes, not the handsome youthful appearance that used to open many doors. He glared at the unwelcome visage.

"What the hell is goin' on with her! Don't I have enough problems with clients drivin' me nuts without her fallin' apart."

Laura woke late the next morning. Ted had already left. As she got out of bed, every bone in her body reminded her of the fall while her mind tried to deal with what she saw on the stairs. She needed a second opinion. A flashback to her recent dinner party caused her to reach for the phone.

"Hello, Aunt Rosie. How are you?"

"Just grand Laura. So nice ta hear yer voice. But ya sound strange girl. Is something the matter?"

"You can always tell, can't you."

"Well I've known ya ever since ya were no bigger'n a pea in a pod."

"I have to talk with you. Can you come over?"

"I sure can, and I've just baked some nice blueberry muffins fer our tea. Put the kettle on and I'll be there in a jiffy."

Laura looked out the front window a short time later to see the sun reflecting off the calm water of the bay. Turning the corner, Rosie's face shone in appreciation of the unseasonal warmth of the December day. Laura was relieved to see that she was now walking without her cane. Incredibly, despite her octogenarian status, Rosie survived the hip operation with flying colors. She put up quite a battle with her doctor to make sure she would get the operation.

"I ain't finished dancing yet," she told him. "All's I need is a little mechanical tune-up. You get er done, and I'll be dancing a jig round yer Christmas tree."

Laura smiled to think that Rosie just might pull it off as she watched the spring in the old gal's step. She greeted her at the door with a gentle hug and a kiss on the cheek.

"Aunt Rosie you look great! I'm so happy to see you walking well again."

"Thank you, my dear. Those lovely girls at the physio were very helpful, put me through my paces, they did. Here, take these muffins and let's have a little kitchen gabfest. I'm glad ya didn't take that ol woodstove out. It makes things right cozy, just like my place."

Laura loved the large, cast-iron stove with the brass fancywork on the front, inscribed with the date 1908. She could picture her grandmother busy in the kitchen preparing bread for the oven. The smell of baking bread would always remind her of those happy childhood days. Even with the modern electric stove installed, Laura still used the woodstove for cooking in the winter. The crackling of the wood fire created a comfort zone in her kitchen, her favorite place in the house.

She took the teapot off to pour large mugs of tea and set them on the old oak table that her grandfather had made.

"I'm afraid Ted wants to get rid of it and put in some kind of gas fireplace instead. Maybe I can talk him out of it." She frowned and muttered, "If he's not dead set on it."

"Well you set him straight. That there's an antique full of memories." Rosie peered over her glasses to scrutinize Laura. She suddenly raised her voice in alarm. "What's happened to yer face? Ted didn't hit ya, did he? Is that why yer soundin' a bit off and wantin' ta talk?"

"No, calm yourself, Aunt Rosie. That's not it. I had a fall last night. I need to know about the woman who has been seen on the widow's walk in this house. I remember you mentioning it last week."

Rosie's eyes started popping. "Why do ya want to know? Did ya see her?"

"Yes, I did. On the stairs, last night. She's the same woman who's been in my dreams." The calmness in Laura's voice was betrayed by the lowering of her eyelids, a trait Rosie knew well.

The old woman's eyebrows rose to form little wrinkles on her freckled brow. She set down her mug and took Laura's hand. "Now don't ya fret none. From what I understand, she's a friendly spirit but is troubled by some tragedy. There's some that thinks she's Charles Lindsay's sister, Emma, who disappeared mysteriously."

"Emma! Her name WAS Emma!"

"Yes. That was her name. It just popped into my head."

"Emma is the one who wrote the letters we found. I was thinking Charles Lindsay was the brother she mentioned. It's all starting to make sense. But why is she trying to contact me, Rosie? It's making my head spin."

"We're goin' ta figure that out. I remember Mary Lindsay, Charles's wife, talkin' about her one time. Broke Charles's heart, she did. There was somethin' she wouldn't tell me though, like 'twas a family secret."

Rosie paused to inhale the bouquet of her tea, then sipped it in deep concentration. She put down the cup, blinking rapidly. "Ya know she left me a little jewelry box when she passed. There was a key in there. I always wondered what it was fer. I'm thinkin' it could have somethin' ta do with the mystery. Is there anythin' in the house that has a lock without a key?"

Laura paused for a moment. "I can't think of anything, but there are some things in the attic that I haven't sorted through. I never liked going up there by myself."

"We'll start there. I'm goin' home ta fetch the key and you can start lookin' fer a lock upstairs. Rosie'll be back ta protect ya, don't ya worry none."

"Don't you want to finish your tea first?"

"No. That can wait. We have a mystery ta solve."

Laura smiled as Rosie scurried out the door. She couldn't ask for a better Watson.

- TEN -

PARTY TIME

THERE WAS NOWHERE ELSE TO LOOK. LAURA WENT TO THE small front window of the attic to let in some chill air to clear away the dust they had disturbed. The old sea chest with its rusted hinges looked promising, but treasures from a sea captain's voyages distracted the ardent sleuths from their task. The real find in the chest were two framed photos. One was a wedding picture of Laura's parents and the other, a picture taken of Laura, her mother and her grandparents, the last photo they had taken as a group before the untimely deaths. She set them aside.

They searched on to try to find chests of drawers with locks. Unopened boxes were also attacked without success. Some lovely linens and lace collars were discovered and put aside for the museum, but the search for the mystery lock had Laura and Rosie stumped.

Heading down to the kitchen, Laura realized with a start that it was already four o'clock and she had accomplished none of the work Ted had wanted her to do. She took some meat out of the freezer to make his favorite casserole and poured herself and Rosie a cup of tea.

They munched thoughtfully on the remaining blueberry muffins suddenly aware that they had missed lunch.

"Guess we'll have ta think on this some more but I just got this gut feelin' that key is goin' ta tell us somethin' about this house."

"I think you're right, Aunt Rosie, but I'm feeling a bit brain dead. I'm going to put it on the back burner and try to get on with some of the work around here."

"You're right dear. Sometimes revelations can come out of nowheres when yer mind is idling or doin' another task. It's just like whenever my memory hits a brick wall, I just lets it go, and bingo, before ya know it, the memory comes through. It's like an old dog diggin' around aimlessly, then surprisin' himself with his lost bone."

The telephone rang to cut off Laura's thoughts. A rich baritone voice cheerfully met her "hello".

"Hi Laura. It's Ray Williams. I'm calling to remind you of the little Christmas party I'm giving for my students and their spouses this Saturday. Also, the departmental scholarships have been announced. I'm happy to tell you that you're one of the recipients. We'll be making the presentations at the party; so, it would be especially good if you are able to be there."

"Thank you, professor. That's great news! I was planning to come, but will have to check with my husband about his schedule. It's such a busy time of year."

"Let's not be too formal, Laura. Remember. Call me Ray. I realize that Halifax is a bit of a drive from Mahone

Bay, so if the weather turns bad, or if you would like to, please stay overnight. I have a large house with lots of rooms. You and your husband would be more than welcome."

"Thank you Ray. That's very kind."

"I'd miss my favorite student if she couldn't make it."

"I'll do my best and let you know later. Bye for now."

"Hope to see you soon. Bye, Laura."

Laura put down the phone and walked slowly back to the kitchen table.

"That's a puzzled look you have on your face, my dear."

"Oh, it's just a little problem I have to work out with Ted. That was Professor Williams inviting us to the student Christmas party at his house. He says I'm being offered a departmental scholarship."

"That's just grand, Laura. Kate and your mama would be proud of ya. What could possibly be the problem?"

"The problem is Ted just told me he wants me to quit my studies."

Rosie sat back in her chair, and started fluttering like a hen ruffling her feathers. "Whoa there, girl! That doesn't sound ta me like a little problem. What's his reasonin'?"

"He thinks I should be concentrating on redoing the house. He's even suggested starting a family now."

Rosie's eyebrows arrowed up with a question. "And what's your feelin'?"

"I don't think he's being fair. I've planned and prepared for this for a long time. I don't know why he's putting pressure on me now to start a family."

"Then stick ta yer path, girl. Take that advice from an old gal who's made a lot of wrong turns. And it's okay ta be angry. I can hear it in yer voice."

"It's also fear. This could cause us some serious problems."

"Are there any marriages without problems? Let me tell ya a few stories about my dear departed Alvin."

Engrossed in their conversation the women did not hear Ted come home. When he peered around the kitchen door they both looked up with a start.

"Well this looks like a kitchen party, ladies. It's a good thing I've brought some party treats," Ted said as he deposited a bottle of dark rum on the table. I have a little celebrating to do." He leaned over and gave Laura a hug.

"What's the occasion, honey?"

"We've been invited to the VP's house in Halifax on Saturday. Usually it's only the firm's partners that are invited. I'm thinking they might be announcing a new partner, namely, yours truly. Put on your best party dress, baby. You're going to impress the hell out of them."

Rosie took one look at Laura, and knew it was time to leave.

"Well my dears, ya'll have ta party without me. This old lady needs ta go home and feed her cat. Let me know if ya need any more help, Laura. Ya know where I'm at."

Laura saw Rosie to the door. When they hugged

goodbye Rosie whispered in her ear. "Be strong. Keep ta yer path."

- ELEVEN -

Fallout

THE FIRST REAL BATTLE IN LAURA'S MARRIAGE LEFT HER weak with anger. Hot tears blistered down her face as she slammed the bedroom door behind her.

How could he be so selfish and insensitive. Didn't he know how important this was to her? The memory of his words prickled like pins in her soft parts. "You're my wife and I expect you to support me in my career. Lord knows I've supported you with this job."

Guess he forgot about the time when he was a student, and she was working, as well as going to school AND keeping house. This was supposed to be her time to follow her dreams. Besides, this was HER house that he was transforming to impress his boss. He seemed to overlook that little fact.

He was not going to have his way this time. If he did not want to come to her award presentation party, she would go alone. Aunt Rosie was right. She needed to follow her own path, even if she had to follow it by herself.

She heard Ted on the stairs and walked over to the door. He would have finished the bottle of rum by now.

She gave the lock a turn.

In the stairwell Ted stumbled and cursed loudly as he cracked his ankle against the hard oak step. Walking unsteadily to the bedroom, he turned the doorknob.

"Laura what're ya playing at. Open the door."

Silence.

Loud knocking and curses produced no results.

"Bitch! I can play this game too," he muttered as he made his way to the spare bedroom. His fingers fumbled along the wall without finding the switch. The only light came from the full moon shining through the window. Flopping on the bed he opened bleary eyes to see a shadowed face framed by a cloud of hair hovering above him.

"That you, Laura? Come here, honey. I forgive you."

When he reached out, two burning coals instead of eyes flared out at him. He started back placing his arms up in front of his face. When he opened his eyes, the face was gone.

"Damn. What the hell was that!" Ted sat up on one elbow and peered around the room. "Must've reflected off the moon or somethin'. Maybe I need to cut down on those after dinner drinks." He eased back down, grabbed a pillow, and put it over his head to block out the moonlight… and any other disturbing visions that might enter his brain.

The next couple of days were as frosty indoors as the weather outside. Ted and Laura moved around each other in a silent charade, each not wanting to be the first to break the silence. Ted had his supper at the local pub, and Laura ate sparingly at the kitchen table as she tried to concentrate on her research.

Inevitably, Saturday arrived, finding them with horns still locked. Ted walked into the bedroom, his fists clenched. "I'm going to ask you one more time, Laura. Are you coming to the party with me?"

Laura sighed, and took a deep breath. "No, Ted. As I've tried to explain to you, this scholarship is a big deal to me. I AM going to be there for the presentation. I'm really disappointed you can't see that and be happy for me."

"You just don't see it. This promotion could be huge for both of us. It's important that we be seen as the happy couple."

"Guess that would be a lie."

"Well I'm leaving. With you or without you."

"Guess it will be without me."

"Have a nice bus ride," he said with a smirk.

As the front door closed with the force of a freight train, Laura felt the surge of Celtic fire in her blood.

He knows there aren't any buses now. He's not getting me with that ploy!

She picked up the phone. "Hi Aunt Rosie. I need to ask a favor of you. Can I borrow your car?"

"Of course, my dear. Tonight is your big night, isn't it? Rosie paused for a moment considering whether the question would be an intrusion. "Ted didn't give in, did he?"

"No he didn't, and he took the car. I need to get to Halifax on my own."

Rosie heard the heat of her words feeling anxiety for the future of their marriage. "Well, just be careful of the roads. I hear there's a storm comin' later."

"Don't worry. If the weather is looking bad, I'll stay in the city." A nervous smile fluttered across her face as she pictured her handsome prof and the possibilities in his offer. "I have a place to stay."

"Do what ya think's best. Just let me know so's I don't worry meself foolish."

Rosie hung up the phone muttering to herself. "I think there's more goin' on in her head than a scholarship party. I just hope she knows what she's doin'."

- TWELVE -

STORMY ROADS

As Laura pulled out of Rosie's driveway her stomach churned in angry knots, just like the swirling dark clouds above.

"How dare he leave me stranded, punished like a misbehaved child!"

Driving towards the water she viewed the usually calm bay whipping white caps to an ever-increasing tempo. She would have to drive quickly to reach Halifax before the storm broke. The weather forecast gave her an eighty per cent chance of getting there before the freezing rain. She urged the aging Volkswagen Beetle that Rosie called Bugsy to its max.

"I know we haven't been friends long, but I know you can do it."

She turned onto the forested highway that is one of the main arteries into Halifax. Skirting the road in inky darkness, wildlife abounded, victims and unwilling causes of accidents. Laura had had several close calls previously with deer and coyotes and watched nervously for the telltale glowing eyes. The forty-five-minute drive seemed much longer at night, with visibility never good enough. Cutting through a blanket of black, oncoming headlights struck her eyes like blinding shards of glass. Chugging a steady beat, Bugsy rattled and shuddered against the whistling crosswinds. Laura tensed near the exits to Halifax. Slowly at first, then like a pounding drum, the freezing rain began. The crackling splatter of ice crystals soon started to immobilize the struggling windshield wipers.

"I must have been insane to go out tonight," she muttered, eyes aching. "But I'm almost there. If I can just get down Ray's road safely."

Feeling the increasing wind pushing against the small vehicle, she thought of the steep driveway down to his lakeside home, and shivered. With the wipers barely working, Laura spotted the house and pulled the wheel sharply to the right. In an instant, she felt the wheels let go of the road. As she tried to ease on the brake, the car skidded sideways.

No control! Turning the wheel only makes matters worse! Hold on tight!

The car began an agonizing three-sixty downhill spin towards a large pine tree, faster and faster and faster. Panic was the last thing she remembered.

When Laura woke up, there it was again – panic…of a different sort.

Why was she on Ray's bed?

"Where am I? What happened?" she mumbled as she tried to raise her head. A shock of pain struck her behind the eyes. Through blurred vision, she saw Ray's concern as he sat next to her gently stroking her hand.

"Laura, I'm so relieved. Take it easy. You've had an accident and a bad knock on the head. Lie still, and try to relax. Are you feeling any pain?"

His voice was softly soothing as she tried to grasp the meaning of his words. "As long as I don't move my head, I seem to be okay. Can you turn down the lights a little? How long have I been here?"

Ray crossed the room to turn off the overhead lights, leaving the table lamp lit. "When I heard the crash I ran out and couldn't believe it was you. You were unconscious. I carried you in about twenty minutes ago. I'm so sorry you didn't get my message postponing the party. I didn't want you to make that drive in the storm. Now that the ice pellets are in full force, nothing is moving. I can't even get you to medical treatment. This is all my fault." He grasped her hand again, distress deepening every line in his face.

"Not your fault that I didn't get your message, Ray. It was my choice to make the trip. I heard the storm was coming. I'll be all right. I'm just a little foggy and belly bruised." She was deeply touched by his concern. Still, the question arose...

Was it fatherly concern or was there some other message she should be reading from those penetrating eyes?

"I called my neighbor, Dr. MacKinnon, and told him I didn't think you had any broken bones. He said to give him a report when you woke up and to keep an eye on you tonight. He wants you to go to his clinic in the morning, whenever the roads are cleared, so he can check for a concussion and any other injuries. Until I can get you there, I'm going to make you as comfortable as possible. First I should find some candles in case we have a power outage. I'm going to build a fire in the fireplace too. Can I get you anything? Water? A whiskey?"

Laura smiled. The answer to her question was becoming clearer. She had never seen Ray behave this way. In her mind's eye, he was always Ray Williams, PhD. That there was another more inviting side to his personality grew apparent with every action, and unless she was badly mistaken, signals of affection were flashing like beacons back and forth between them!

As exciting as that thought was, she decided to try to keep her beacons in check, just in case he was only being protective of a young female student. Her grasp on reality was a bit shaky lately.

"Some water would be good, thanks Ray. I think I had better try to reach my husband. I don't know the phone number that he's at right now, but maybe I can leave a message at home in case he's back or calls the machine."

"Don't worry Laura. I'll look after it. Lie still and rest."

Ray returned in a few moments, and gazed at her outstretched form on the bed. A sadness passed over him unexpectedly. He brought a glass of ice water to her bedside, his thoughts in another world.

Laura caught the change in his face. "Is something wrong, Ray?"

"No, it's nothing. I was just thinking how long it's been since I've shared this room with a woman."

"Since your wife passed away?"

"Yes. That was two years ago."

"How did she die?"

"Breast cancer. She put up a brave fight but it was discovered too late. She was too young to die."

"It must have been horrible for you. I'm so sorry." She reached out to take his hand. "I do understand this type of loss. It can leave you lonely and empty."

"Do you believe in an afterlife?" he asked searching her face.

"A month ago I would have said no, but now I'm not so sure."

"What changed?"

Laura hesitated, deciding in the end that she was not sure how he would receive her ghost story. "Let's just say moving back into the house where my mother grew up and where I spent a lot of my childhood put me in touch with my roots and the connections of family. I feel very close to them even though they have all passed on. There must be something beyond."

"Let's hope so. I've always regretted the fact we didn't have children. It never seemed like the right time. Now I have nothing left of her but memories."

"No one can take those away. Time is a healer if we let it be."

"Hey, shouldn't I be the one consoling you after your injuries! I didn't mean to get into morbid topics. Get comfortable and I'll get the fire going. I'm sure we can find more pleasing things to talk about."

Ted entered his hotel room and searched through the mini bar. Time to celebrate he thought, even if he had to do it by himself. Laura missed one helluva party all right. So, he didn't make partner. So what. The big news was that the firm was expanding. His day would come. Maybe in the Cape Breton office. Guess he should give her a call to see if she's stopped pouting.

No answer. Just the fuckin' answerin' machine. Can't even leave a message. The fuckin' tape is full because she never fuckin' clears it! Where is she?

After an hour of fuming and several stiff drinks later, he decided to call home to check the messages on the machine for clues.

Scrolling down to today's messages he finally got the first one: "Hello Laura. This is Ray. I'm sorry to tell you that I have decided to postpone the celebration until next weekend due to the weather. There's no way I want you to be driving in the ice storm. Talk to you soon."

Message Two: "This is Ray Williams. Laura is staying at my house for the night. Don't worry. All is well. She's in good hands…

The message ended as the tape ran out.

I just bet she's in good hands, you pervert! Laura, ya fuckin' bitch, I'm done playin' yer games. I have games of my own ta play.

Eyes blazing, Ted took one look in the mirror, ran his fingers through his copper curls, then swaggered out the door heading for the bar.

- THIRTEEN -

REFUGE

LAURA OPENED HER EYES AND TRIED TO CLEAR THE FUZZY feeling in her head. This place was not familiar. In the corner of the room, fireplace coals still sparked reflecting off a brass-framed screen. From between shimmering blue curtains, a weak display of sunbeams filtered through departing clouds. The serene surroundings took on a more intense hue when she turned. On the blue brocade bedspread, barely touching her arm, breathing deeply, Ray Williams lay sleeping.

She froze. No need to wake him. Studying his face intently, she admired the ruddy features dominated by a strong jaw and sensuous mouth. The graying temples belied, yet enhanced, the youthful face. Long lashes fluttered as he slept. She could not forget the penetrating blue eyes.

She tried to piece together the change in her mental and physical feelings. Even though her body ached from the accident, arousal, brought on by his nearness, took over as the dominant force.

The previous night was dreamlike with candles lit

around the room, the fire crackling. This man, that she had placed on a pedestal and had presented himself as an aloof academic, had revealed a soft, caring underbelly. He had also been scarred by grief with a loving relationship lost, a sensitive side of his character that brought them closer.

He was comfortably used to looking after the needs of another. After performing the usual tests for a concussion, and feeling satisfied it was unlikely, he gave her an oversized pair of pajamas to wear and left the room until she was snugly tucked under the feather duvet.

Until he was sure she was not in danger, he sat on the bedside chair, and entertained her with stories of his travels. While the wind lashed the windows with icy sleet, he took her to the sunny shores of Mexico.

"I've been to other southern countries, but somehow Mexico has captured my heart from the mountains and the canyons to the deserts and the tropical rain forests. It's a huge country of great diversity and contrasts; but it was more than that. It was the warmth of the people I met. They opened their doors to me and made me feel welcome even though my knowledge of Spanish was minimal. I think I could live there some day."

Laura was intrigued. "Tell me more of your special places. I have never been in a tropical country." That was all the encouragement he needed. Laura became spellbound.

The ancient Mayan ruins and the mysteries of the

temples of Teotihuacán opened her inner doors of wonder, awakened the longing in her to explore other cultures and to experience sunny climes. She fell asleep imagining the pounding of surf from a bamboo hut on a palm-lined beach.

Now with the morning light, she must face the many cold questions buzzing through her head about her present reality.

She had to call Rosie. Were the phones working now? How badly was the car damaged? But it was Sunday. How would she get it repaired? She should call Ted. Did he get home? Were the roads okay now?

Just as she was thinking that she should wake Ray, he opened his eyes, rolled over to face her, and smiled his perfect smile.

"Good morning pretty lady. Guess I fell asleep. Had to make sure you were okay through the night." He reached over to take her hand. "How are you feeling now? How's your head?"

The unaccustomed compliment and the touch of his hand raised her heartbeat a notch above normal. Trying to control a sudden nervousness, she paused her response with short breaths. "Uh, my brain seems to be coming around. Just, uh, feeling a little achy and bruised."

Ray reached over to gently touch her face. In a huskier voice, he leaned closer and said "I wish there could be another way of getting you into my bed." Sighing deeply, he kissed her forehead, "Tempting as this is, I think I should get you over to the Doc to get checked out."

As he helped her out of bed Laura felt a pang of disappointment and thought, "If those beacons of affection flash any brighter, they could blind me completely."

In a hotel room in downtown Halifax Ted opened his eyes, then quickly shut them to repel the stabbing daylight. A sultry voice filtered through the pounding in his head.

"Are you awake, sweetie? I should go. My shift starts in an hour. Hope you're not hurting too bad. That was quite the bender you laid on last night. I'm just leaving my phone number here on the table. Maybe we can hook up another time."

Ted lifted his head and tried to focus on the departing redhead.

Great legs.

"Yeah, honey. Good times. I'll see ya."

What the hell was her name?

Ted sat up shakily. The memories were beginning to drift back, then the anger surged.

I wonder where that slut of a wife is now. Still with Doctor Know-It-All? Guess I'll have to find out.

He reached for the phone.

- FOURTEEN -

Wounded

Laura rose to clear away the breakfast dishes. Ray had borrowed a tracksuit from a neighbor that fit her reasonably well. The party dress she had worn did not seem appropriate for her doctor's visit. He was now outside sanding and salting the driveway. She watched him through the kitchen window as he bent and tossed the sand effortlessly, admiring the strength of his muscular body

The jangle of the telephone interrupted her thoughts. Perhaps it's the doctor calling back.

"Hello. Ray Williams residence."

"So, you're still there. Finished whoring, yet?"

"Ted? What're you talking about?"

"Two can play at this game. Let me tell you about my night. I connected with one helluva redhead that knows all kinds of kinky turn-ons. So, you and your Doc have fun. I'm having mine."

"Ted. You've got it wrong," Laura shouted into the dial tone. She raised her hand to her forehead trying to quell the oncoming torrent, then looked up to see Ray in the doorway staring at her.

"Laura, are you all right?"

Angry words burst out of a chest full of hurts.

"How can Ted treat me this way? I've never been unfaithful to him, ever. I'm so tired of these false accusations. It's just an excuse for him to…to…" It was too hurtful to say. Only tears spilled out.

A breath of crisp winter air from Ray's jacket filled her nostrils as his arms wrapped around her, building a warm, safe cocoon where she could hide and forget. With her emotions in a whirlwind, she was finding it difficult to think rationally and could only babble out Ted's accusations.

Ray's calm strength seeped into her like a tonic. She followed his logic and direction as if being guided out of a wilderness. "The first priority is to get you over to the clinic. We don't want to take any chances with a head injury. I'll call the road service to get the car towed over to my mechanic. I had a quick look, and it doesn't seem too bad. It just needs a bit of bodywork. You call your aunt and tell her you'll be staying here until you've had your injuries checked out, and the car is fixed."

Laura faced him as if to protest.

"And don't even think about Ted. Even if you could contact him, he's painting his own scenario, and nothing you can say right now is going to make a difference. I know the type, a hothead of the worst order. Wait until he cools off. You can make your peace then." He paused to look into her eyes. "If you want to."

Her voice choked as she struggled to hold back yet another flood of tears. "I don't know if I do."

Ray pulled her back into his strong embrace stroking her back gently. "One thing at a time, Laura. You know you can count on me. But right now, you've a doctor's appointment to keep."

Doc MacKinnon peered over his oval reading glasses revealing warm brown eyes shadowed by furry grey brows. "Hello Laura. I understand you've had a bust-up with a pine tree and came out the loser. Tell me exactly what happened and I'll have a look just to make sure there's nothing nasty lurking about."

His voice had a soothing effect with a tone of genuine concern. She liked him immediately. "I lost control of the car going down Ray's icy driveway. The little Beetle was spinning in circles before it smashed into the tree. I hit my head and my stomach is sore. Ray said I passed out for about half an hour."

"How are you feeling now? Any headache, nausea, or pain in other parts of your body?"

"Yes, a bit of a dull headache. I feel bruised, mostly around my middle where the seatbelt was. There's some pain in my neck but I don't think there are any broken bones."

"Get up on the examination table. I'm going to check you over and examine your eyes with a light."

He felt her neck, shoulders, then her abdomen. She winced a little with the pressure.

"I don't think there's anything broken, but you'll likely be sore for a few days." He leaned towards her to shine what resembled a light pen, first in one eye, then the other. He straightened, and walked back to his desk, sitting down slowly as if the day had been a long one.

"Have you ever had any dizzy or fainting spells, not able to keep your balance, anything like that?"

"Well, I did have a fainting spell a couple of weeks ago." She didn't dare mention the ghost. "I may have been over-tired."

He began writing on a requisition form as he spoke in a soft voice. "You know, I'm a cautious man. There may be nothing to worry about, but just to make sure, I want you to have some x-rays taken of your head, neck and abdomen. The office will make an appointment for you. Leave a number where we can reach you." He gave her a wink. "Make me happy. Come back to see me as soon as you can afterwards. Ibuprofen should work for those aches and pains. Let me know if it doesn't."

Laura left the doctor with her mind racing. *Where would she be?* She left two phone numbers with the clerk, Ray's and her home in Mahone Bay.

I don't have time to worry about this. It'll just have to take a back seat to everything else that's going on.

She put on a smile to greet Ray as he stood up in the busy waiting room with eyes searching her face. After helping her navigate the still slippery walkway of the clinic, and settling her into the car, Ray turned Laura towards him. "What did the Doc say? Everything okay?"

She loosened her seat belt. "Yes, nothing to worry about. But you know doctors. He wants me to take some x-rays, just to make sure."

"Make sure you do it. I was able to call my mechanic. Your car will be ready tomorrow. I'm going to keep you captive until then. You need some thinking time." He started the car. "Don't worry. I'll be good." His smile did not convince her, but it was a warm and caring look that beamed at her.

"Okay. I guess you're in charge, but I need to stop at a drug store to pick up a few things.

"It's really you who's in charge, you know. Shopping center coming up."

It felt good to have someone concerned about her needs. She suddenly realized that this was the missing part in her marriage. Life with Ted had been a series of events enhancing his career, his desires. Now, when she needed his encouragement and support, it only led to arguments and unjustified jealousy. She never knew how to deal with his anger, and there was always an underlying fear that the anger would manifest itself physically. Although, maybe he knew that she would not stand for that. There was no question that physical abuse would give her a one-way ticket to walk out the door. Emotional beatings, his strong suit, just left her helpless.

Her head hurt. She leaned back on the car headrest, closed her eyes and felt Ray reach over to squeeze her hand. When they arrived at the house she tensed up going down the steep driveway once more. A brief muscle spasm singed her nerves. But the sand and salt had done its job; there was no problem with Ray's heavy 4-wheel drive vehicle.

Another cog turned in her brain.

Rosie! She still needed to call Rosie!

Even after she told her about Bugsy, the voice of her aunt was like a cool cloth on her forehead. "I'm so relieved ta hear from ya, girl. I heard the storm was bad, shuttin' down the roads and the phones, but I had a feelin' ya were holed up somewheres safe. Don't ya go worrin' about that ol' car none. It's already had nine lives and I just use it ta do me shoppin'. I'm sure it's still goin' ta be good fer that."

"I feel bad about it, Aunt Rosie. I wasn't very smart to drive into Halifax with that storm threatening."

"You hush now, never mind. I'm just glad ya weren't seriously hurt. Now I've some news that will cheer ya up. Our search for the place where that key fits may be over. I remembered that Mary donated her roll-top desk to Reverend Darcy for the church when she died. I'm thinkin' the key may fit in there somewheres."

"That's a great idea! There are often hidden compartments in those old desks. We'll get onto that when I get back."

"When are ya gettin' back? Where are ya stayin' now?"

"I'm staying at Ray's house, my prof."

"Oh, it's Ray now, is it? Does Ted know about this? Where is he? No one seems ta be at the house now."

Laura could visualize her aunt's kindly face puckered up like a big question mark.

"Aunt Rosie, it's a long story. We'll talk when I get back in a couple of days, after the car is fixed. You know I love you."

"I can't wait ta hear all about it. Love ya too, dear."

Laura put the phone down, and wondered what she could tell Aunt Rosie when she, in fact, hadn't figured it all out herself. However, the mystery of the key might be just the diversion she needed, as the bricks of her marriage and her plans for the future, were all tumbling down around her in a chaotic pile.

- FIFTEEN -

Restless Night

Ray tossed and turned in the spare bedroom on the second floor. Sleep was elusive as thoughts drilled through his brain. He had tried to be the perfect host, the kindest friend, but below the surface there was a seething chemistry about to erupt.

He knew she felt it too. He was sure of it. Each time she visited his office he could not ignore those low-cut sweaters, long muscular legs in short skirts and a smile that would melt concrete. When she walked in the door, he dared not look into those large gold-green eyes. It was hard to concentrate on anything other than her beauty.

But she is more than a beauty. Her mind is sharp, flowing to the core of issues without effort. He enjoyed their shared laughter when they came across something historical that was absurd in today's context and appreciated her indignation at the way women were mistreated in the past, without equal rights.

Being her uninvolved supervisor challenged his moral fiber.

I must hold back. Can't let things get out of control.

Tenure is just around the corner; the university does not look kindly on affairs with students. But she's not an immature undergrad. She's a mature, married woman.

Married – the other problem, even worse. He would have to wait. Let her make up her own mind. But how could she stay with that bastard of a husband? She's too smart to put up with his abusive nature. He's a time bomb ready to go off. He better not lay a finger on that precious girl, or he'll have me to deal with!

He beat the pillow with a clenched fist, then rolled over on his back eyeballing the digital clock as he turned.

Midnight! He had to get some sleep. Classes tomorrow morning begin at 9:00.

He shut his eyes tightly, but her image was still there – the angelic face with luscious lips, the body he longed to press against his own, the enticing breasts he longed to kiss. There was no controlling the desire throbbing unmercifully under the sheets, hard as an oak post.

It had been such a long time since he felt the warmth of a woman's body. It was time to put grief aside. Damn! It would be easy to seduce her now. She's so hurt and needy of affection.

The internal struggle continued for another hour until a winner emerged.

No, not yet! She must be free to come willingly. I want more than a one-night stand. She's worth waiting for.

Sleep was his reward.

In the bedroom below, Laura reached over to the other

side of the bed, and felt the emptiness. She didn't like sleeping alone. She longed for a warm body to give her comfort...but not any body. It wasn't Ted she longed for. It was the handsome, charming, intelligent, caring man in the bedroom above her who was stirring long-lost emotions.

She heard the floorboards creak. Was Ray restless as well? It would serve Ted right if she went upstairs and fell into Ray's arms right now. Ted's hurtful jealous rages had killed the love she once had. His words stung her like poison nettles buried deep. She didn't have the energy to deal with all the conflict anymore.

Why was the man who had vowed to love her treating her this way? Now he was screwing around! Did she have to worry about AIDS and sexual diseases, too!

The anger consumed her, stealing her sleep. She arranged the pillows once more trying to find a comfortable position for her aching neck. Her arms got in her way whichever way she turned. Finally, on her back, she tried to focus on her breathing yoga-style, concentrating to relax her body.

I need to rest. There's that x-ray appointment early tomorrow morning. Strange how they got me in so quickly – a worrying thought she didn't need.

She sighed.

If she had more nerve she would knock on Ray's door. There would be relief in his arms.

He had been the perfect gentleman. This was so unexpected. As the hot prof on campus, he could easily be a womanizer. It wasn't the right time for her to be involved with anyone, but she couldn't help visualizing the feel of his muscular body thrusting against hers. She wanted to taste his mouth and wrap herself around him like another skin. The thoughts tantalized her erogenous zones with fiery sparks of pleasure.

It had been such a long time since lovemaking had been satisfying. Would he refuse her? How awkward if he did. He is her prof. She didn't need any ugly complications. She had never been unfaithful before. But he is SO tempting!

The battle raged back and forth, until weariness flowed into sleep like water cascading over a cliff.

The morning sunshine brought reality in focus as Ray and Laura went through the motions of eating a quick breakfast. Both avoided eye contact to hide those secret midnight thoughts that did not fit the sobering daylight.

Yet Ray could not help but notice how even a simple tracksuit showed off Laura's curves, and how the sunlight reflected off the golden curls framing her face. He cleared his mind and awkwardly cut the silence.

"I'll drop you off at the hospital before heading to class. I'll be finished by four. The car should be ready, so if you meet me at the office we can get it then. Let's plan to grab a bite to eat before you head back to Mahone Bay."

Laura hesitated but finally locked into the blue sky of his eyes, "I want to thank you for all you've done. You've been great. But I really need to get back after I get the car. There may be word from Ted, and Aunt Rosie will need her car."

The corners of his eyes creased with a smile, disguising his disappointment. "No thanks necessary. Just glad I could help. Like I said, you can always count on me."

Laura flashed a look of gratitude trying to suppress the excitement she was feeling at the intensity in his voice. "Guess we better get going."

After her x-ray appointment at the hospital, Laura walked along University Avenue towards campus. Stopping at the Nova Scotia Archives, she decided to try to do some research on her project; it would help pass the time until Ray was finished his classes. She found it difficult to concentrate.

Christmas break started tomorrow. The thought depressed her. She had tried to decorate the house, but her heart was not in it. With all the renovations going on, Ted had said that a tree would just get in the way, that they had not accumulated many good tree ornaments, and that they should not spend money on that kind of foolishness right now.

Every year Christmas brought a deluge of happy/sad memories: her parents' loving faces as they shared a glass of mulled wine, decorating shortbread cookies with Gran, the smell of turkey sizzling in the shining wood stove she loved so well, aromatic pine boughs decorating the staircase, and a magnificent pine tree almost touching the high ceiling. She had loved helping with the tinsel, and putting on her homemade decorations that mother had carefully saved from year to year. Aunt Rosie was always there to tell stories and spoil her with candies. Rosie was all that remained of those good times.

What would greet her now in that house? An angry husband? More arguments? Or worst of all, the possibility of a naked redhead! There was nothing there to greet her but gloom…. and a ghost trying to warn her of something. At least, according to Aunt Rosie, the ghost would not harm her.

- SIXTEEN -

VISITATIONS

TED WALKED CAREFULLY UP THE ICY STEPS OF THE PORCH, and unlocked the door. Reaching for the light switch, he peered into the darkness at what appeared to be a white nightdress floating on the staircase landing. A strong scent of lavender hung in the air irritating his sinuses. He hated lavender. When the light from the entranceway chandelier brightened the hallway below the landing, the vision disappeared.

"Laura you home?" His shout echoed back from the stairwell. Silence.

No one there. His eyes were playing tricks on him again. He never liked being in this house alone at night.

He walked over to the answering machine and pushed the delete button. As the whirring tape rewound he scanned the living room. The fireplace was not completed and the patchwork on the walls was only half done.

Dammit. There's nothing happening here. The workmen probably arrived with no one to let them in. I can't count on her for anything! Where is that bitch? Still playing house with lover boy? I've got better places to be.

As the car peeled away towards his favorite watering hole, Bugsy's headlights flashed onto the famous steeple of St. James Anglican Church.

Laura always enjoyed the scenic entry to Mahone Bay with the three church steeples all in a row like sentinels facing the imposing ocean. As she passed St. James, she suddenly remembered Darcy's desk, and Rosie's message. Visiting him tomorrow with the key would be the priority. She could put her worries aside for a day.

There was no car in the driveway. Ted was not back. She was relieved.

Even though it was still early, all she wanted to do right now was crawl beneath the down-filled covers of Gran's big bed and sleep. She would call Aunt Rosie to see if she could drop the car off tomorrow, and to ask her to make plans to see Darcy.

She would also lock the bedroom door.

As Laura fell into a restless sleep the soothing scent of lavender drifted in from a gentle world of dreams. She was a child again staring at the shining star on top of the Christmas tree, and wishing she could open her presents. Gran came into the room with a plate of shortbread, still warm from the oven. A tall lady wearing a long black dress came with her. Her face was covered with a dark veil, but her eyes shone warmly through the netting, and shining black curls glistened on her shoulder.

"Laura I want you to meet, Emma. She will stay here

for a while. She has a present for you. You can open it now, but first you must promise to always listen to her."

"I promise, Gran. Oh, thank you, Miss Emma." Laura eagerly unwrapped the small parcel tied with a red ribbon. Her eyes blinked in puzzlement. "It's a key. What's it for?" Laura reached out to grab Emma's hand. She was leaving.

Before vanishing through the solid oak door, she turned. Laura heard the unspoken words.

"Your real present must be unlocked by the key. Wait no longer."

Thunderous knocking on the very same door brought her back to consciousness like a cold-water shower. "Laura, let me in. You've got some explaining to do, you slut." Fists continued their pummeling.

Laura groaned. "You're drunk, Ted. I'll talk to you when you sober up. Go away." Still groggy with sleep she rolled onto her sore belly, and put a pillow over her head.

"I'll go away all right. Don't you worry about that. Don't think I won't. But this isn't over!" Ted leaned heavily against the door. Exhaustion was winning the battle. His eyes were blurry. He followed a dim light hovering in the hallway to the spare bedroom. He flopped onto the bed without undressing.

The light followed him into the room. It grew brighter forcing him to open his eyes. The intense smell of lavender hit him again as if he were sprayed by perfume, causing him to cough. Its taste nauseated him. When he could focus, a screaming face jumped out at him, growing larger and larger in the center of the light. Flaming eyes glared like missiles from Hades. As the light fired brighter, long fingers reached like eagle talons threatening to claw his face.

"What in hell! Get away from me!" Ted shouted panic-stricken. Rolling off the bed to avoid getting clawed, he swatted the air with both arms and legs, like a cat on its back. The light suddenly left. He forced his eyes wide open, heart pounding. Nothing was there, only total blackness, and the sensation of ants crawling all over his skin.

The noise woke Laura out of her dream state once more. At first it was difficult to determine whether the shouts were real.

Where's that coming from?

She switched on the light, and unlocked the door looking cautiously into the darkness of the hallway.

Ted's shadowy form rushed out of the far bedroom as if pursued.

"You can have this bloody house with its freakin' ghosts. I'm fuckin' outta here!" He stumbled down the dark stairwell, eyes bulging, heart drumming, hands fumbling for his car keys. He didn't bother to lock the door or grab his coat.

- SEVENTEEN -

ROSIE GIVES ADVICE

Rosie looked out her kitchen window to see Laura pulling up the driveway. She immediately bustled over to the stove to put on the kettle. They would have time to have a cup of tea before going over to Darcy's. She needed to talk with that girl to scope out what on earth was going on. While doing her daily chores that morning, thoughts had been buzzing around her head like a dozen deerflies, and landing from time to time with the sting of worrying possibilities. She took a good look at Laura getting out of the car.

Her head shook from side to side, as she talked to herself, the long grey braid swinging like an angry cat's tail. "Land sakes, she looks plumb tuckered out. I've never seen her look so pale. Look at the bruise on her cheek and the bump on her head! That better be the accident and not her man's doin'. If it's him, he'll have the wrath of Rosie ta deal with, and that ain't pretty."

She opened the door, and grasped Laura in a ma-ma-bear hug kissing the side of her good cheek. "Dear girl, I've been so worried. Ya look like ya been drawn through a knothole. Sit down, have a cuppa, and tell Aunt Rosie all about it."

"I'm okay, Aunt Rosie."

She didn't like the weary tone of her voice. "That's not the face or the sound of an okay girl." Her navy-blue eyes scanned Laura's expression like a laser.

"It's just a lot of things are happening I don't understand." Laura sighed and breathed into the warmth of the teacup.

"Well, start by telling me about yer injuries."

"They happened because of the accident when the car went out of control in Ray's driveway. It was just a bump. I had it checked out by a doctor."

Rosie's face relaxed. "That's good. But what is it yer not understandin'?"

Hesitating, Laura considered Rosie's intent gaze and knew there could be no holding back. She would persist until all was told. The words rushed out of her dammed-up emotions in a torrent. "It's Ted. He's just acting crazy. Calling me names. Drinking too much. He called to brag about sleeping with some red-haired woman. Last night he stormed out of the house cursing, saying he wasn't coming back. I don't know where he's gone. Frankly, I don't think I care anymore."

Tears came spilling out as Rosie drew her close, stroking the hair that ran in an unruly current down her back.

"My poor girl. I'm so sorry. Ya don't deserve this. Do ya know what set him off?"

"It's his jealousy. I stayed the night at Ray's during the storm, and he thought there was something going on."

Rosie pulled back and looked her in the eye. "Was there somethin' goin' on?"

"No. He was a gentleman, very kind." Laura sipped her tea once more, afraid to show her more.

Rosie's eyebrows arched up as she rose to fill the cups. She thought for a few moments before replying. "I'm kind of an old-fashioned gal when it comes ta marriage. But, ya know, when I consider what I've seen, and what ya told me, I wouldn't blame ya if ya did fall for this Ray fella. Tell me about him."

Laura cleared her throat and thought for a moment. "He's a very caring, intelligent and interesting person. He seems to like me. We have a lot in common. But he's my prof. That's awkward for both of us."

"Would ya be interested if he did make a move?"

Laura couldn't help but smile at Rosie's directness. "Well, he also happens to be gorgeous."

Rosie smiled in response, enjoying the gleam in Laura's eyes. "Sounds like ya've already made up yer mind." Then she put on her serious face. "In this ol' lady's opinion, there's just one thing ya've got ta ask yerself. Do you still love Ted? I don't need ta hear the answer. It's fer you ta think about."

She got up to shuffle her slippers towards the hall closet for her coat and boots. "Right now we've got ta go over ta see Reverend Darcy before he heads inta Lunenburg fer the day."

Laura looked down at her hands, and twisted the wedding band that now hung loosely on her finger. What had happened to the man who vowed to love her forever, who swept her off her feet when they were at university? They had met at a party and she was immediately attracted to his chiseled features and athleticism. The attraction was mutual. They both played on the basketball teams, which started their conversation. He made her laugh with his stories of summer jobs in the lumber camps and his impressions of the local dialect. When they danced together for the first time it was as if a magnetic force was at work drawing them closer and closer together.

He paid his own way through university. There were no silver spoons in his rural upbringing as the son of an Anglican minister with a drinking problem, and a mother who had abandoned the family when he was in high school. He left to work in Halifax, then entered university, driven to succeed. Being an architect was his dream, and hard work was never an obstacle for him. Ambition had been part of his appeal. But now it swallowed them both, and spat her out.

Jealousy was another matter. Why did he react so strongly? Or did he just need an excuse to mess around? He was too young for the mid-life crisis. No! Damn it! There was no valid excuse for his behavior.

Rosie watched Laura brooding and tried to read the thoughts that rolled over her like a thundercloud. This decision would take time. It should not be rushed. Rosie concluded that a change of pace from all the turmoil was what Laura needed.

"Listen, my pet, I know there's a lot on yer mind, but we have a mystery ta solve. I've got the key in my pocket. Let's go have a look at that desk."

Laura suddenly sparked. "Yes, I almost forgot. Before Ted left last night, I had the weirdest dream. Emma gave me the key as a Christmas present, then told me not to wait any longer."

Rosie blinked owl-like. "Emma?"

"Yes, in my dream."

"Come, child. There's no time ta waste when a ghost gives directions."

- EIGHTEEN -

A Treasure Is Found

His impish face beaming with pleasure, Darcy greeted Rosie and Laura at the church hall like long lost family.

"Laura I've missed our little visits. They brought some sunshine into my dreary basement office. Rosie you're looking as spry as a spring heifer. It's good ta see ya runnin' about."

"Thank ya Darcy. Yer as full of the blarney as ever, but, yes, that new hip made a new woman outta me. I'm just full of piss and vinegar these days."

"I can attest to that," Laura piped up.

"Some things don't change," he chuckled as he led them into the office, and sat down at his desk. "Now I understand ya want ta have a look at this old roll-top desk that Mary Lindsay donated ta the church. I've been using it ta write on when I prepare my sermons. Is there something ya want ta know about it?"

"Well, ya see, we have a little mystery ta solve. Mary left me a jewelry box when she passed, and there was a small key in it. We're wonderin' if it might fit some hidden place in the desk."

Darcy sat up in his seat. "That's very interestin'. I'm a man who loves mysteries, but I've never thought ta check for a hidden compartment. Let's investigate." He began clearing off papers.

Laura stroked the smooth oak finish. It had been well looked after. "Is it okay to empty the drawers, Darcy? I've heard there's sometimes a false back creating a hidden space."

"Why, sure. No problem There're mostly old sermons and writing paper in them. I'll give ya a hand. Rosie why don't ya poke around the upper part of the desk ta see if ya can find anythin' suspicious."

The three sleuths attacked the desk with enthusiasm. While Rosie rummaged through the small upper compartments checking for false bottoms and keyholes, Darcy and Laura emptied the drawers, pulling each one out of its slot, one by one, starting at the top. They looked at the rear of each drawer to see if the full space was open to view and checked the back for any secret entryway. After four disappointing searches, they opened the bottom right-hand drawer.

Laura sucked in her breath. "Look there's about a five-inch space at the end that's not showing." With difficulty, she pulled the sticking drawer all the way out. A trembling voice called out to Rosie "I think we've found it! There's a small round keyhole at the back."

Rosie dove into her pocket and handed her the key.

Three sets of eyes watched hawk-like, as Laura turned the key and pulled down the carefully crafted door. Wedged tightly inside, a bound book, grayed by age, had the name Mary Hicks Lindsay printed neatly on the cover.

"Saints alive! We've found a treasure," Darcy exclaimed. "Open it girl."

"I just knew that key was important," Rosie chortled taking a position at Laura's other shoulder, reaching for the reading glasses hanging from her neck.

The cover crackled with age as Laura turned the page. "It looks like a journal starting with Mary's marriage to Charles Lindsay. There's a genealogy of Mary's family and that of her husband Charles at the beginning pages. There are some photos and letters tucked in the back, too."

Laura immediately scanned the Lindsays until she came to Emma. Her name had an asterisk beside it and read Emma Marie Lindsay, born February 15, 1898, deceased September 10, 1918, married to Edgar Harkness, May 16, 1915. Under Emma was the name Katrina Mary Burgess, born September 10, 1918, father Andreas (Andrew) Burgess, below in brackets adopted by Maurice and Suzette Dauphinee, January 20, 1919.

Laura's hand dropped, still holding the book.

This was the message Emma had sent her. It suddenly made sense. She was meant to find Mary's journal, the key to Emma's story.

Her shocked eyes full of questions darted at Rosie. "Did you know all this time?"

"Did I know what?"

"That your friend, my Grandmother Kate, was not a Dauphinee. She was a Burgess, adopted not long after her birth, daughter of Emma and her lover, Andrew!"

"Emma the ghost!"

Laura nodded. "She's my great-grandmother, my other gran."

Rosie sat down and blinked several times. "Well I never!"

Darcy held up the finger of one hand, and scratched his head with the other. He burst out in a strained squeaky voice. "Now wait just a minute. I'm missing some facts here. What ghost?"

Rosie and Laura caught the comical expression on Darcy's face, bulging eyes darting from one to the other, full of fear, yet yearning to know more. They couldn't help laughing.

Rosie patted his shoulder. "Don't ya be worryin' none, Darcy. Emma's a fine ghost and we'll tell ya as much as we know."

"I need to borrow this, Darcy. Maybe it has the rest of the answers I'm looking for."

Laura's focus now became clear. Her mission was to search out the facts and be the narrator of Emma's story. Their connection was strong. Emma was driving her onto a new path.

She returned home to find a message from Ray on her answering machine telling her of the new date for the

Christmas party and presentations. She would have to tell him that her thesis would be on hold until she could get Emma's story written.

Would he understand? But how could he? It all sounded too crazy!

Perhaps it would be best to tell him she had decided to stop her studies for the time being. She would try to reach him tomorrow. Right now, she had a journal and photos to explore.

- NINETEEN -

THE WRITING BEGINS

THREE DAYS LATER ROSIE WALKED THROUGH THE UNlocked front door and found Laura sitting at the kitchen table nibbling on a muffin, sipping her tea, and closing the final entry of Mary's journal. She was concerned to see her still in her robe, hair uncombed, dark circles under her eyes, looking like sleep was a distant memory. It was not like Laura.

She looked up, as if coming out of a trance. "Oh, hi Aunt Rosie."

"I just let meself in, dear. Ya must not of heard me knockin'. Yer phone's not workin'. I thought I'd check ta see if ya were still alive."

"Sorry. My mind has been kinda locked on this journal."

"I've been waitin' ta hear. But look at ya, pale-faced and eyes poppin'. Have ya not slept since ya left us?" She bustled over to the kitchen counter, sniffed at yesterday's half-eaten, tuna sandwich, and dumped it in the waste basket.

"The journal has possessed me. I couldn't put it down."

Her voice rose as she spilled out the words. "I know their story now. Mary was Emma's confidante and friend. I'm going to write the story as if it were happening to Andrew and me. Emma's blood flows through my veins. I know she wants me to do it, and she'll inspire me along the way. She told me so in a dream last night."

As she scanned Laura's earnest face, Rosie's brow furrowed. She placed her hands on her hips. "Are ya sure ya want ta do this, child, or is't the devil's doin'? Yer actin' like yer possessed."

"I know it's a little crazy, and I can't explain it, but I really don't have a choice. Besides, everyone deserves to have their story told, especially when it has all the drama of a Shakespearean play. Don't worry. I'll survive."

She pulled two sepia photos out of the back of the journal and placed them in front of Rosie. There was excitement in her voice. "Look at these pictures. I can finally see the faces of the two lovers."

Rosie put on her glasses to study each one. "They certainly made a handsome couple. He has the clear eyes, strong chin, and blonde hair like so many of the German folk in this area. I can see how she would fall fer him. She has the look of the Irish, a dark-haired beauty, small in stature, but wiry with a bold stare. Yes, she'd be a force by my reckonin'. She must have somethin' important that she wants ta deal with ta still be hangin' round this house."

"I wish I knew why she is pushing so hard."

"I'm sure she'll be tellin' ya when she's ready. I'll be

lookin' forward ta reading that journal when yer done with it, but just you remember ta keep yer head above water. Ya have a life ta lead too. I'll be checkin' in on ya now and then, but right now I'm goin' back home ta call the phone company so ya can call me if there's any problem with that ghost. I don't like ya stayin' here by yerself. And by the way, any word from that snake of a husband?"

"No, but the phone has been out for days. It must have happened during the last storm. It doesn't matter. I'm not in the mood for any more of his jealous accusations."

Rosie shuffled towards the door in her stocking feet, brow still furrowed. She sat on the bench near the entranceway to put on her boots. "Remember I'm just around the corner, and Darcy is nearby. And I'll be expecting ya fer supper."

"Thanks, Aunt Rosie. Don't worry. I'll be all right."

When Laura heard the door close she faced her typewriter wondering where to begin. The history of the time, the writings of Charles and Mary Lindsay, the letters, the photos, and the visitations from Emma's ghost were the tapestry of Emma and Andrew's story. She knew she could make it all work, but there was so much to tell.

Of course! The beginning HAD TO BE the eventful day of their first encounter.

- PART TWO -

Emma's Story

Characters in Emma's Story:

Emma Lindsay Harkness - The ghost in part one

Ginny and Lily - A mother and child rescued by Emma

Edgar Harkness - Emma's husband

Mary Lindsay - Emma's brother's wife

Charles Lindsay - Emma's brother

Peter and Liz Baker - Mary Lindsay's parents

Andrew (Andreas) Burgess - Emma's lover

Robert Burgess - Andrew's brother

Louisa Burgess - Andrew's mother

Katrina - Emma's baby

Maurice and Suzette Dauphinee -
Couple who bought the rectory from the Lindsays

- TWENTY -

THE MEETING

HALIFAX, NOVA SCOTIA - DECEMBER 6, 1917

Enjoying the sunshine in the crisp morning air, Emma swung her arms to keep warm. She made her way to the Halifax market, taking a scenic route along the bottom of Citadel Hill where the historic fort overlooked the city, separating north from south. Even though she loved her seaside hometown of Mahone Bay, the bustling city of Halifax was exciting. She had been more than willing to accompany her sister-in-law, Mary, on the visit to her aging parents. They lived near the new Camp Hill Hospital, now busy with wounded soldiers from the war. The women were surprised that Mary's parents, despite their age, were very active in the hospital's auxiliary, organizing volunteers, and finding comforts for the wounded. The visitors were quickly recruited as volunteers in the wards. Mary's experience as a midwife was particularly useful since she knew how to change bandages and could find a way to ease the pain of the broken with her healing hands. Emma followed Mary's compassionate lead in this endeavor, even though her stomach churned when viewing the disfigurements caused from the battlefields. This morning's walk to market on an errand gave her an escape, and she breathed the cool air deeply, cleansing the images from her mind.

She was on the south side of Citadel Hill, when the unthinkable happened. A deafening roar vibrated through her body throwing it to the ground as if flung by an angry demon. Stunned and barely conscious, her ringing ears picked up sounds of glass shattering, structures tumbling, and heavy objects falling from the sky like a rain of rocks. She curled her body into a fetal position trying to protect her head and face with her arms. While her mind tried to come into focus, her eyes started to fill with grit and her lungs labored with the heaviness of smoke. From a lofty mushroom cloud, a dark, oily haze descended onto the city bringing with it the acrid smell of burning buildings, burning flesh. Bits of greasy debris began to cover her like a black, evil snow.

Head still spinning, she staggered slowly to her feet. As the ringing in her ears subsided, the distant cries of pain, horror, and grief began to pierce through the gloom - sounds from an unimaginable nightmare.

What has happened on the other side of the hill!

When she scrambled up the incline to get a better viewpoint, her mind numbed with disbelief. Half the city destroyed! The north end, as far as her eyes could see! A growing wall of fire was developing along the Narrows!

Ships of every description were lying scattered like broken toys!

Dropping to her knees, body trembling, she grasped for possible causes.

Had they been attacked by the Germans? Had a submarine gotten through the harbor defenses?

The harbor and Bedford Basin were full of navy and supply ships developing convoys to aid the war effort. From the beginning of the war, residents had been living with a fear of bombings and enemy attack.

Were they still in danger? Should she be taking cover?

She climbed higher to see if she could gather any clues. From the height of the hill the full force of the disaster lay before her. The area of the city known as Richmond was flattened with no building standing. Elsewhere houses were in various stages of collapse, some on fire, twisted lumber and metal scattered everywhere. Sounds of minor explosions were still going off. The biggest devastation lay at the Narrows where the Bedford Basin empties into the harbor. Amidst shattered dockside buildings, a large cargo ship blown out of the water, listed helplessly on the shore.

Emma cried out in shock and despair "Oh, the people! There must be thousands killed and hurt!" As she strained to see through stinging eyes, blackened shapes staggered through the wreckage, their tattered clothes hanging from bleeding bodies. Some called out names in panicked voices, some stood stunned in front of a heap of rubble, some sat moaning and sightless picking at glass in their eyes. One man stood completely naked, staring around with dark eyes, as if awakening from his dreams to find himself in hell.

She started to run down the hill towards Gottingen Street. Military vehicles and ambulances were picking their way through mangled automobiles and upturned wagons attached to dead horses. Several horses that survived raced white-eyed over debris fleeing fires, pulling empty carts. Semi-torn residences suddenly burst into flame as the exposed fireplaces, recently warming the family hearth, fed on the waste around them. With horror-filled eyes she stepped over sooty body parts tinged with dried blood. Nothing she had seen in the wards prepared her for this madness.

There had to be something she could do. Where to begin?

As she got closer, the sounds of the wounded wrung her heart, but above it all she heard with woman's ears, the sound of a baby crying. It came from her left where a once two-storied wooden home was caved in, as if a giant hammer had slammed down the middle. All the windows were gone. The remaining walls jutted out at broken angles. Cautiously, she entered through a doorway with its door hanging loosely on one hinge and peered into the half-light of the living room. A moan drew her attention away from the infant cries towards the fallen timbers. Amid broken planks of wood, a small woman lay crushed by a giant beam, her legs and belly pinned where it angled down from the fallen ceiling. Her darkened face, framed by a nest of tangled auburn hair, was contorted with pain.

"Oh, dear God! Don't worry missus. I will help you. What is your name? Is that your child I hear?"

"Me name's Ginny. Me babe…Lily…in the back kitchen."

Emma rushed to the back of the house to find a young baby in its carry cot near the heavy iron wood stove. The walls around the cot were still standing encircling the untouched infant. It was a miracle of survival in a cauldron of devastation. She quickly decided Lily's cries for relief could wait and hurried back to Ginny.

"She is fine, Ginny. Do not fret. First, I must see to getting you free.

Emma strained mightily at the beam with all the strength in her small frame, but there was little hope of moving it on her own. She ran to the broken window and shouted from the tips of her toes, "Help! Someone please help! There is a woman trapped in here." She shouted long and loud, and wept to hear the woman's continued moans amid the baby's cries.

Just as she was about to give up and go in search of assistance, a shadow appeared in the doorway. A tall, lean man walked into the dim light. As he moved to Emma's side, a kind and gentle face peered from beneath a woolen cap. Intelligent eyes took in the situation immediately.

"Oh thank God. Whoever you are, you have answered our prayers."

"The name's Andrew. I think we can do this, if we work together. On the count of three I'll lift the beam while you pull her out." The deep, bass voice was calm and reassuring, overpowering the unnerving distress heard in the baby's continued cries.

"I'm Emma, Andrew. Yes, I know we can do it. We must." She bent her slim body over the woman's shoulders. "Be brave, Ginny. This may be painful. We are going to get you free now."

Emma was amazed by how easily Andrew lifted the beam while she tugged at the groaning woman to ease her out. Once freed, Ginny blinked up into Emma's face with moist eyes. "Thank you both. I never tho't I'd see me sweet babe agin. You must save 'er too. In the cot….in the kitchen."

"It will be fine, Ginny. You try to breathe easy. We'll get you both looked after."

Emma begged Andrew with pleading eyes. "Can you go find someone to take her to hospital, while I make sure the babe is all right."

"Yes, of course. I will be back as soon as possible."

"Thank you Andrew. You are a saint. I could never have managed without you."

His parting smile touched Emma like a warm summer breeze. "I am far from a saint, Emma, but I AM very glad to meet you, and to be of assistance."

As she made her way to the kitchen she softly said to herself, "I am glad too, very glad."

- TWENTY-ONE -

Hazardous Journey

HALIFAX, NOVA SCOTIA - DECEMBER 6, 1917

Andrew returned within the hour with a horse-drawn wagon. It was put into service to carry the injured across the city to Camp Hill Hospital. Emma helped him lift the woman onto the cart next to a man suffering from severe burns to his hands. He lay inert with eyes closed, and jaws tight, as if paralyzed by the day's grim reality. Emma turned to Andrew with questioning eyes.

"He was trying to pull his children out of their burning home," Andrew said with a face lined with soot and pity. "None of the three babes survived."

Emma looked away trying to swallow down the bile from her contracting stomach muscles. She turned back to the house and with a strained voice called out, "I am going to get Lily. At least there is one Richmond child who will see another day."

Andrew followed, and helped her with the small cot and the babe who had found a comforting fist to suckle. "I will go with Ginny and Lily to find them some care,

Andrew."

"There are teams searching through the rubble to find more survivors. I will join them," Andrew said, helping them onto the wagon. He withdrew his hand slowly from her arm and looked at her earnestly, "But I am sure we will meet again, Emma."

Emma's cheeks flushed crimson as she fell into the crystal lake of his gleaming, azure eyes. She dared not linger there. "Yes, I hope so. We must do what we can right now. Thank you so much for your help, Andrew. Farewell, and take care for the fires."

By this time other victims had found their way to the wagon including a thin man stripped naked by the blast, shivering under a found blanket. Reeking of smoke and burnt hair, he babbled to no one in particular with owl eyes in a charcoal face, lips parched and cracked. "I was just standin' on deck in the harbor lookin' at the flames. Then the flash came and took me. Up I went tryin' ta swim through the air and slow meself down. Not a stitch on me when I woke up on Needham Hill, near half a mile away." He bent over and held his head, then stared up with wonder. "I am thinkin' hard why I have been saved… when so many poor folks died."

The wagon lurched forward behind the sturdy haunches of a large, black Clydesdale. The uncomplaining beast had eyes wide with fear as it breathed the smoke, but it responded faithfully, stepping carefully around the debris, as if to avoid jarring the broken and bleeding on board.

Emma cradled Ginny who was in and out of consciousness. They had not gone far before a screaming mob of humanity reached their ears. Shouts of "Get out of my way! Hurry! The magazine hill caught fire! Another explosion is coming!" spiked the anxiety of the conscious on board the wagon. It was where the Navy stored munitions for the war. In short time hundreds of people scrambled and pushed by them heading south towards open ground at the Commons or Citadel Hill. The injured or weak who fell were trampled in the panic.

The horse reared up, ears back with nostrils flaring. The driver handed over the reins and jumped down to talk gently to the frightened animal. "Whoa, easy, my beauty. We can do this. We need you big fella." When he could grab the harness, and pat the horse gently, the jangled nerves of the animal subsided. When the bulk of the mob passed, it seemed eager to go on. This time at a faster pace. The passengers now faced a long journey through Armageddon, all the while fearing that another explosion was imminent.

When they finally arrived at Camp Hill, Emma entered a medical nightmare. The hospital was overflowing. The only space that remained for victims was the floor of the corridors. Nurses and doctors worked urgently to assign priority for the neediest. Surgeons worked without stopping to eat or rest. Soldiers who were partially recovered gave up their beds and tried to help those they could. (It was later reported that the 280-bed hospital admitted 1400 patients that one day.)

Dauntless, Emma grabbed a nurse she knew who was rushing by. "I need help for a woman whose lower body has been crushed by a beam. This is her young babe who is hungry and wants care."

In a voice beyond weary, the nurse replied, "Bring her here. I'll see if someone is free to look at her. Your Mary has set up an emergency nursery and is looking after the infants at the school down the road. You can take the babe there."

She got some assistance to bring Ginny in and laid her on the corridor floor near the nurses' station. After what seemed like hours of rocking the fussing infant and getting Ginny to drink some water, Emma was relieved to see a cot coming.

The nurse gave Ginny something to ease her pain while she waited for a doctor. "We'll look after her now. You take the child to the school. Mary is arranging for volunteer wet nurses to help out."

Emma stepped carefully around the moaning and the bleeding in the crowded corridor to leave the hospital with Lily. At the door, a tall man in grimy clothes and hands wrapped in rags was carrying a young girl in a school uniform covered in ashes. Half her face was burned and the hair singed from her head.

"Can someone please help this girl? We dug her out

of a destroyed building." The tired voice was deep and familiar. The face was a map of ash-spattered soot.

"Andrew, is that you?"

With a flash of recognition, a thin smile emerged. "Emma! Can you help?"

"Wait here. You look like you will fall over at any moment. I will find someone to help her." Still clutching Lily, Emma ran to find the nurse who helped Ginny. Her response was difficult to hear but held some hope.

Emma returned to find Andrew lying in the corridor, holding the hand of the disfigured girl whose mouth twisted in pain. Emma spoke softly with liquid eyes. "She will have to wait. No one is available to handle more burn victims. The nurse will be here soon with some pain medication."

Andrew's eyes turned steely hard, and his voice became a whisper. "She can't die now. She was meant to live. We found her buried, and saved her."

"There is hope, Andrew. Supplies and doctors have arrived by train from Truro, with more on their way from nearby towns. The hospital has been notified that a fully equipped hospital train is on its way from Boston. In the meantime, the military hospital ship in the harbor, *USS Old Colony*, can take some of the most urgent patients. The nurse will try to get her there with others that can be moved. You have done your best. Others will help. Don't despair. I have also heard that the rumor that the Magazine Hill was afire is false. We have nothing to fear from another blast there."

His eyes shone with more than gratitude. "Thank you, Emma. I hope to see you again."

She squeezed his hand and met his gaze briefly. "I must take this babe to a nursery, but I'll be back soon."

- TWENTY-TWO -

Mary's Views

HALIFAX, NOVA SCOTIA - DECEMBER, 1917

Mary looked around the school basement and tried to visualize what else could be done for these lost and wounded children. Her mother's friends and neighbors had responded generously with their time and the much-needed supplies. Now soldiers were delivering donations brought in from the trains and repairing the windows of the school so that heat could be maintained.

The cruel winter storm that followed the next two days after the explosion added misery upon misery. Dedicated search parties worked under bitter conditions to find those buried in the snow-covered debris. Many more victims died. As if this were not enough, the heavy snowfall was followed by a heavy rain turning the snow into slush which froze shortly after. The weather gods had no mercy.

Under these harsh conditions, the military and civilian volunteers worked diligently to try to identify the living and the dead with hopes of reuniting families who had been separated. Many children had been brought in for treatment without identification or records of where they had been found. The infants were the most difficult to identify. Sometimes they were the only surviving members of their families. Bodies that were found were placed in the mortuary set up at the Chebucto Street School. Desperate people walked through looking at the charred remains in search of loved ones. Only the strongest were able to bear witness to these heartbreaking scenes.

She wondered how Charles maintained his faith in times like these. He would have received the telegraph by now telling him that she and Emma were fine and had decided to stay to help. She would not want him to worry. She knew he would also be working hard from the rectory in Mahone Bay to assist in aid efforts.

Her medical skills as a midwife were put to use, as well as her organizational expertise learned from administering parish matters. Managing the school nursery was now her responsibility, with her family and Emma her primary assistants. She took charge of fifteen of the unclaimed young children who had been found and treated. Many with serious injuries were still in hospitals. The dear hopeful eyes, searching the faces that entered the school, shredded her heart by times. Any means to give them some comfort and distraction was her immediate goal.

She examined her charges. Infants were sleeping

oblivious, toddlers were rocking themselves to remembered tunes clutching blankets, and the older ones were huddled in small groups in a trance-like state. What was to become of these poor waifs now? The Richmond protestant orphanage had been destroyed killing staff and all but one child.

Mary's thoughts were interrupted by Emma's return, her arms loaded with baskets of clothing and food. Why was she smiling? Good news would be welcome.

"Mary, the train has arrived from Boston! There are doctors, nurses, and medical supplies including a team from the Red Cross."

"God bless them all! Our hospitals desperately need relief. I don't know how they have managed to keep going. And look at you, child! You look like you have fallen in a flour bin. There is no blood in your face at all. Sit down and rest."

"I am fine, really, just a bit winded." Emma gazed briefly into Mary's face and then blinked away hesitating.

"What is it, dear?"

"I have a favor to ask."

"You know you can ask anything of me."

"Well, as you know, the city has thousands of people homeless now. I know your parents have taken in two friends from Richmond. Do you remember the man I told you about who helped me with Ginny and Lily? He has been helping at the hospital and has nowhere to go at night except the bitterly cold tents set up on The

Commons. He is from the Lunenburg area and was staying at a hotel near the north end train station that was destroyed. He has slept little since the explosion. The poor man is exhausted, but wants to continue helping. Do you think they could find him a bed until he can make his way home?"

"I am sure they can. I will ask when I go back to the house. My sister and I are planning to take turns staying at the school with the children until other arrangements can be found; so we can share a bed. There will be a spare room for your friend. Tell me more about him."

Mary watched Emma's face carefully as she told her more about his rescue of Ginny and Lily. The color returned. There was a glow about her that she had not seen for some time.

"His name is Andrew Burgess. His brother is fighting on the front. He is very proud of him and is close to his mother. He became her sole support on the farm when his father died recently. Since the explosion, he has worked tirelessly to search for survivors. I have been at the hospital helping to register the victims and have seen him various times as he brought people in. I think he is an extremely kind man."

Mary's eyebrows raised as she thought how impressive this must be to Emma after what she experienced with her degenerate husband.

"And I suppose he is handsome as well?"

Emma visibly blushed this time. "Well, yes, I guess he

is, in a rugged sort of way. Do not tease Mary. You know I have a husband."

"Yes, more's the pity. Fortunately, he's away most of the time. When is Edgar's ship returning?" She watched a cloud pass over the recent radiance in Emma's face.

"Next month," she murmured as she walked over to Lily's cot to check on the sleeping babe, placing a blanket over her.

"You are in charge. I will be back soon," Mary said. "I am going to the house now to ask my parents about Andrew."

Mary bent over to pull on her boots. She tucked in the dark wisps of hair that fell from a loosely-wrapped bun before covering her head with a shawl, then smoothed her skirt down from her round body. She marched out into the cold briskly. Angry thoughts sped her along. She was glad to have Emma living with them at the rectory, but she had no time for Edgar Harkness. He often abused Emma verbally, and she was sure she heard the sound of slaps coming from their upstairs bedroom. She would never forgive herself and Charles for allowing the marriage to take place. They were her guardians, but they had been fooled by him. They had failed her. He had better be on his best behavior when he gets back, or Charles will be dealing with him. She would see to that.

- TWENTY-THREE -

THE BAKERS MEET ANDREW

HALIFAX, NOVA SCOTIA - DECEMBER 10, 1917

Mary watched from the porch of her parents' spacious three-story home on Jubilee Avenue. She had been inspecting the makeshift shutters that covered the shattered windows when she heard Emma's voice making a happy, laughing sound. It was music to her ears. She turned smiling to see Emma walking down the street with a broad-shouldered man wearing a knitted cap and heavy woolen jacket. A canvas duffle bag was slung on his shoulder. He held Emma's arm firmly to steady her on the icy walkway. As they climbed up the steps, his azure gaze captured her attention, as did the firm jaw that mellowed into an easy smile.

Emma made the introduction like she was offering a special gift. "Mary, this is Andrew."

He grabbed Mary's hand firmly. "I am very pleased to meet you and extremely grateful for the offer of accommodation. Emma has told me of all the good work you and your parents have been doing. Please let me know if there is any way I can assist."

"Pleased to meet you as well, Andrew. It seems you have been busy enough with the rescue work, but I will bear your offer in mind. Come in and meet my parents. From all that Emma has told us, they are looking forward to having you here."

Waiting in the hallway, Peter and Liz Baker bubbled with welcome and curiosity. Peter reached up to pat his shoulder. "Our Emma has told us how you have been working with the rescue teams, lad. Happy to have you in our home."

"Thank you Mr. Baker. You are all very kind to take me in like this."

"Not at all, not at all" chirped in Liz with a lilting Irish accent. "I've fixed us a nice pot o' tea and some scones. You sit yerself down and tell us all about yerself."

"Now Lizzie, give the lad a chance to catch his breath. Emma take him up to his room. When he's ready he can come back and sit with us a spell."

Andrew followed Emma up the winding staircase to the third floor. The tiny room had been a maid's quarters and was sparsely furnished. He placed his duffle bag on a small trunk near the bed.

Emma drew the heavy curtains to block the draft from the closed shutters. "This is my room when I am in town. I will stay in Mary's room. It is a little chilly up here with the windows still unrepaired, but there are plenty of warm blankets on the bed."

As she moved towards the door Andrew took her hand and drew her closer to him. "I will be just fine since I will be nearer to you. You have made this disaster bearable. I want to know everything about you."

Emma was captured by the clear longing in his eyes, but her own yearning had to be subdued. It was too dangerous. Reluctantly, she looked down, and pulled away. She picked at the lace around her sleeve with nervous fingers. "I am fond of you Andrew, but there is something you must know." Her eyes were unable to hide their sadness. "I am not a free woman. My husband is at sea. He will be returning next month."

The lines around his mouth grew taut as he searched her face. "Are you happy with him, Emma?"

She turned away, closed her eyes and replied with a deep sigh. "Please, do not ask. I am not able to do anything against Edgar."

The agitation he saw confused him. "Forgive me. I meant no offense. I did not know."

"I take no offense, none at all." She smiled weakly. "But we should join the others for tea."

They returned to a kitchen gathering immersed in debate. Details of the explosion were surfacing. Blame was being shot at the captains of the two colliding ships that caused the disaster.

Peter Baker paced the floor in angry strides. "There'll

be hell to pay for this. The French ship *Mont Blanc* came into the harbor without warning that it was loaded with volatile munitions. Even after the collision the crew on the Norwegian ship, *Imo*, watched *Mont Blanc*'s people abandon ship thinking it was because it was sinking. They should have thought again when they saw the captain leave too. People came in to fight the onboard fire without knowing of the danger. It is unconscionable that so many people died in this city while most of the crew of the *Mont Blanc* survived by making their way to the Dartmouth shore."

"Now Peter, don't get yer English feathers all in a curl. There's blame to be had on both sides in how the ships came together. There was a harbor pilot on board the *Mont Blanc*, and some said the ships were goin' too fast. Other ships in the channel caused confusion. Signals were not read properly. The court of inquiry is seeking out witnesses. It'll all be sorted. In any case, naught to be done now but mop up the mess."

"And a bloody mess it is too," Peter fumed determined to have the last word for once.

Liz turned to see Andrew and Emma listening in the doorway. "Come in and join us, my dears. Ya must be exhausted. There's a nice cuppa and some nourishment comin' yer way. Mary get us one more chair from the dining room."

"Thank you Mrs. Baker. That would be most welcome, but please, let me get the chair," Andrew replied, moving quickly to the dining room.

"Tis Liz, dear. Just call me Liz." She watched with admiration as he lifted the heavy wooden chair with one arm and joined them around the kitchen table. "Now, tell us more about yerself, Andrew. Our Emma says yer from the Lunenburg area. What's yer father's name?"

"His name was Andreas Burgess. His great grandfather immigrated to Canada from Germany in 1753. My family farm is near Blue Rocks. Father died a year ago. My brother, Robert, is away in the army, so it is just my mother Louisa, and I living there right now. I was in Halifax taking care of some business when the explosion happened."

"Were ya able to let her know yer all right? She'd be frettin' on ya."

"Yes, I was able to send word to her via the telegraph office in Bedford."

"Mary and Charles have been living at the rectory in Mahone Bay for the past five years. Are ya familiar with St. James Church?"

"Yes, it is along the shore as you come to the bay from Halifax. It is a very beautiful setting. I am quite familiar with Mahone Bay. Some of my relatives on my mother's side are in the shipbuilding business there and several are sailors."

"What are their names?"

Mary interrupted. "Now Mother, you're sounding like the local constable. There's no need for an interrogation."

"Oh, I'm just bein' a busybody. There's sure ta be people we know in common. Tis a great pity that some folks have been harassing anyone with a German last name, blaming them for the disaster and such. They are just plain ignorant of our Nova Scotian history."

Mr. Baker chimed in, "Yes, I have heard some very disturbing stories of property damage being done. Disgraceful!"

Alarm in Andrew's face caused Liz to quickly add, "I'm sure yer mother will be fine where she's livin'. It's the Halifax riff raff causing the trouble."

An awkward silence caused her to change the subject. "Now, Emma's husband, Edgar Harkness, sails out of Mahone Bay, as did her father, before his ship ran aground at Sable Island." Noticing Emma's downcast eyes, she reached over to pat her hand. "Bless his soul. He was a good man. Alas, Edgar was the only one to survive that shipwreck."

Mary grumbled to herself as she cleared the table. "It is a great pity the good get taken, when the mean and miserable get left behind."

Hearing the words, Andrew's eyebrows shot up.

Was this the meaning behind Emma's comments? She is not able to do anything due to his nature?

Later Andrew tossed under the blankets of his newly acquired bed in the Baker garret. After the makeshift tent in which he had spent several days, it was warm and comfortable despite the draft. Nevertheless, his weary body could not turn off the churning thoughts that possessed him. This was the bed that Emma had slept in. He could almost feel the firm softness of her body, and smell the dark tresses that formed a cloud around her sweet face. They have known each other for such a short time, but never had he felt such a strong attraction nor such a strong connection to another person, man or woman. There was an unexplained magnetism between them. Her eyes told him he was not alone in his feelings, but she hesitated. Her marriage vows bound her to another. Her loyalty was admirable, but from Mary's comments, it appeared that the union was not a happy one. He could not bear to think of her being abused. He must learn more about Edgar. If he were indeed a villain, one way or another, there would be a rescue. With this thought, his mind relaxed enough to allow a fretful sleep.

- TWENTY-FOUR -

Andrew Gets Advice

HALIFAX, NOVA SCOTIA - DECEMBER, 1917

The chaotic relief effort progressed as civilian and military forces united to save survivors and start to rebuild. Much-needed supplies were brought in by train from across the province and from other areas of Canada and the United States. Able-bodied people in the city were assigned tasks related to the care of the wounded and the homeless.

Andrew, Emma, and Mary found themselves working closely together with homeless victims who were searching for lost family members. It was a time of emotional swings - from the depths of sorrow in the makeshift morgues to the heights of joy when parents were reunited with their children. Sharing the elation of each small victory and the sadness of each tragic loss, the dedicated threesome grew closer every day.

Andrew and Mary walked together towards the Nova Scotia Technical College where a supply depot had been set up for the hospitals. They had volunteered to obtain some newly-arrived medical supplies that were urgently needed for the children's ward. Andrew at last had the opportunity he was waiting for to have a private conversation.

"Mary, I hesitate to ask you, but I am deeply curious and concerned about Emma's relationship with her husband. She says little about him. I fear all is not well."

"Too right. He has revealed himself to be a drunkard and a bully. He talks to her as if she were his personal servant and punishes her for any disobedience. She is terrified of him. If they were not living under our protection at the rectory, I do not know what would happen to her."

"She is so remarkable. How did she ever end up with such a man?"

"She was a young and gullible girl of sixteen when she met Edgar. He was full of seafaring tales that made himself out to be grand and adventurous. She romantically thought that because he was the sole survivor of the shipwreck that took her father, he was somehow saved to look after her. The foolhardy girl has had to pay dearly for that mistake. As her husband, he now has control of her small inheritance. Charles and I, as her guardians, should have seen through his lies." Mary's short legs moved her round body awkwardly from side to side as she picked up the pace, fists clenched in her pockets.

Even though Andrew had longer legs, he struggled to keep up with her angry strides. He raised his voice so she could hear "But why does she not leave him?"

"I have urged her to do so, but she fears what he might do. His temper intimidates her. Besides, he has every legal right to take her away with him, or leave with her money. At least now, she has some refuge living with us. Thank the Lord he's away at sea often."

Now sure of her friendship, Andrew confided, "Mary, you know I have feelings for her."

She stopped to look him in the eyes. "Then know that you are playing a dangerous game. These things are not easy for women. I know she looks at you like a knight in shining armor and has feelings for you as well. Love may conquer all, but Edgar will use every devious means and resource to keep her."

Andrew returned the steady gaze. "Thank you for that warning. Be assured that I want nothing but the best for her and will do all I can for her happiness."

Mary hunched her body against the wind blowing up from the harbor. "I believe you will, Andrew, but be careful. He consorts with unsavory characters in Mahone Bay. I trust him not."

- TWENTY-FIVE -

Phone Calls
And Messages

MAHONE BAY, NOVA SCOTIA – DECEMBER, 1985

The chattering phone broke Laura's trance-like state. Three days went by with little time away from her typewriter. Her sleep had been restless, interrupted by vivid dreams of Emma and Andrew. She thought the call might be Ray or Rosie. Both had left messages on the machine. It was time to make contact with the real world, but the call gave her a jolt she was not expecting.

"Hello Laura. This is Mike MacDonald from Ted's firm. Is Ted there?"

"No, he isn't."

"He hasn't shown up for work for the last three days. Can you tell me where I can reach him? There's a rather urgent matter with one of his clients."

"Sorry, Mike. I don't know where he is. He stormed out of the house a few nights ago, and I haven't heard from him since."

"Oh, I see." His voice was hesitant, irritated. "Well,

when he does get in touch can you please tell him to call the office right away."

"Sure. I'll let him know."

Laura's mind flooded with angry thoughts.

He's probably drinking with his red-haired hussy in some sleazy motel. He can stay there for all I care. Not like him to miss work though. He must be on a real bender.

Perhaps she had missed Ted's call. She pushed the button on the answering machine to get her messages.

"Hi Laura. Give yer Aunt Rosie a call so she knows you're alive."

The deep voice in the next message sent sparks through her erogenous zones as she recalled the warmth of the last encounter.

"Hi Laura. It's Ray. Just wanted to remind you again about the party. I have rescheduled it for Friday. Doc MacKinnon's office called, and he wants to see you on Friday at 4:00. You can come here afterwards and stay over, if you like. Call me. I'm worried about you."

How could his voice inspire such a reaction?

It must be the love story she was writing. The romance had excited Laura, awakening a desire she was trying to suppress, a desire not only for the heat of Ray's body, but for the love that had left her life. She thought her love for Ted would be forever, but in the last few years, harsh words and jealousy had emaciated that love until it was a skeleton of broken vows. To love, honor and cherish had disappeared from their daily lives.

It would be foolish to be loyal to a skeleton.

She made her first call.

"Hi Aunt Rosie. It's me. I've been so involved in writing that I've forgotten to call you. Sorry."

"Good ta hear from ya. I want ta read Emma's story and the journal if yer done with it."

"You can have the journal soon and you will be among the very first to see the final story, but it will take some time yet." She paused for a moment.

She had to do it.

"I need another favor. Can I borrow the car this weekend? I have a doctor's appointment and the scholarship party on Friday."

"What's with the appointment?"

"Oh, I'm sure the Doc is just wanting to talk about the x-rays."

"No word from Ted yet?"

"No. He hasn't showed up for work either. The office just called."

"That's a bit strange. Will ya be staying at Ray's again?"

There was no getting anything past Rosie. "Yes. I think so. He has invited me to stay."

"Make sure yer clear in yer mind about what yer doin', girl. The car is no problem."

"Thanks, Aunt Rosie. You're the best."

Laura braced herself for the next call, but was disappointed to get Ray's answering machine. She left a message. "Hi Ray. It's Laura. Sorry I didn't get back to you, but I've been immersed in a writing project I want to discuss with you. I'll see you after my appointment Friday, and yes, I would like to stay over for the party."

Friday seemed like a long way off. She needed to get back to her writing to make the time go more quickly. Besides, with Emma's nightly invasion of her dreams, the love story exploded in her imagination. She could feel the passion building.

- TWENTY-SIX -

Emma's Dilemma

HALIFAX, NOVA SCOTIA — DECEMBER, 1917

Emma brushed the hair back from her face, and stood up stretching her back. The past weeks had been exhausting. She looked around the empty schoolroom that she was using to sort out the information that had been gathered and realized that her labors here would soon be over. She was relieved, yet each day taking names down in her register and hearing the stories of the lost and injured gave her very little time to worry about her own problems. They are surely small compared to those on her register, she would admonish herself. And yet, she must face the inevitable return of Edgar and her feelings for Andrew. Each evening Andrew waited to walk her back to the Bakers. He insisted the streets were not safe at night with the military still patrolling for looters. Mary was making herself scarce of late, excusing herself from joining them, knowing this was their one opportunity to be alone.

How much closer she felt to Mary than her brother, Charles, who was 15 years her senior. He was always kind, but took his role as her guardian very seriously. Even though she had married two years ago, he still felt protective. She could not face disappointing him. He had set an impossible example of goodness that she strived to emulate. If she abandoned her husband to run off with this wonderful man, it would not reflect well on Charles, a minister in the community. Divorce was not possible for common folk like herself. Mary would be affected by the gossip as well. But more upsetting was the thought of Edgar who would surely go after her. He would do harm to all who aided her.

She recalled his last jealous rage when a shopkeeper dared to call her by name and held her hand a little too long. Edgar rushed forward pushing Emma out of the way. He grasped the impish man by the arm, twisting it halfway up his back. "Unhand my wife, you swine. It is Mrs. Harkness to you." He threw him down to the ground and kicked him roughly in the side, then turned around to glare at Emma. "And you, missus, stop your wanton ways, or it'll be you gettin' the thrashing next."

She was too mortified to ever enter the shop again, even though it sold her favorite sweets.

Although she longed for his touch, the thought of Andrew being harmed could not be endured. Never had she been so desirous of a man. She avoided his eyes, fearing that those warm gazes could dissolve all her noble resolutions. Soon they must both return to Mahone Bay to a life she could no longer abide, now that she knew a man like Andrew.

It was all madness. She was dreaming of the impossible.

A gentle tapping at the door disrupted her thoughts.

"Emma, it's Andrew. The caretaker let me in before he left. He asked if you would lock up for him. Are you ready to leave?"

She stood and turned towards him. His presence in the midst of her dilemma seemed like a message. She wanted to tell him how she felt but her heart was vibrating so strongly the words fluttered in her throat unable to escape.

He walked quickly to her side and took her hand. "Emma, what's wrong? You look uneasy. Have I upset you?"

Gathering courage, she lifted her face, damp with tears. "Dear Andrew, how can such obvious affection upset me? And yet it does, because I must not respond."

He brought her hand to his lips. Then brushed her hair from the wetness of her cheek. "Emma, do not be afraid. I know about Edgar. Mary told me of your life with him. You deserve so much better. Know that my heart is yours, and trust that I will be your protector, whatever happens."

His deep voice and tender words released the caged emotions she could no longer withhold. They were the key to unlocking all the unhappiness that trapped her. As he bent to kiss her lips, resistance dissolved into a river of passion that swept through both of them, at first like a gentle stream, but as their bodies fell against each other, the stream flooded into a raging torrent.

She felt him firm and throbbing as his muscular legs pressed against her thighs. Now she fully understood the term wanton, because every part of her wanted him, wanted all of him, deep inside. His long probing kisses that moved from her lips, to her neck, to her bare and heaving breasts kindled a need so primal there was no control she could possibly enforce. Clothes were quickly shed as they embraced into an urgent union of ecstasy. She opened herself to feel his manhood press her pleasure regions in a pulsing blissful union. She held him deep until an explosion of white light and sound consumed them both, sparkling through every part of their bodies.

Waiting for their heartbeats to return to normal, they lay on the floor together panting, not wanting to move. He pushed up onto one elbow and gazed at her with liquid eyes. She reached up to gently touched his cheek. "Oh, Andrew, what have we done? This is sheer madness. We cannot go on."

"Know that I cannot go on without you. I love you. If you wish it also, I will find a way for us to be together."

"But Edgar…."

"Hush, my love, I am not afraid of Edgar. He is just a bully and no match for my feelings for you."

- TWENTY-SEVEN -

Emma's Return

HALIFAX, NOVA SCOTIA - JANUARY, 1918

Emma and Andrew made the best of their last weeks in Halifax. Their time together was as unnerving and powerful as the explosion that had rocked the city, with each day increasing the fear of their return to Mahone Bay and the difficulties that would follow. Separation was impossible to contemplate.

They were distracted for a time with preparations for Christmas. The Bakers had rallied their hospital volunteers to make a cheery dinner for the staff and patients of Camp Hill Hospital. By a stroke of luck Peter Baker had commandeered a supply of turkey from his contact at the naval base. Baked goods and treats were prepared by the ladies under Mary's direction. Emma and Andrew scoured the shops that were open to find small gifts for the children and collected contributions from the neighborhood. With the help of the hospital staff they were pleased to be able to bring some small measure of joy to the occasion.

As the day of their departure drew near, Emma clung to Andrew's words: *I will find a way for us to be together.* Yet she knew that Edgar would be waiting for her at the rectory. Sitting on the bed with downturned mouth, she watched Mary finish packing belongings for tomorrow's train journey. Mary knew her too well for her to be able to hide the feelings brewing inside. She needed the support of her friend more than ever.

"Mary, what am I to do? I love Andrew. I cannot go back to Edgar."

Straightening her shoulders and placing hands on an aching back, Mary lifted her head and suddenly shared another pain, the pain in Emma's face. She knew it would be difficult, that Charles would say sacred vows must not be broken. But there was nothing sacred in Emma's marriage to Edgar. With his brutal treatment of her, Edgar had broken every vow. She must support Emma in hopes of some resolution. Charles did not need to know, not yet. She sat next to Emma and put her arm around her.

"You are strong, my girl. Wait to see what Andrew can do. In the meantime, neither Edgar nor Charles can know... for the safety of all." She gave her a squeeze. "You have an ally in me, no matter what happens."

"Mary, what would I do without you?" Emma whispered and fell teary-eyed into her soft embrace.

Andrew decided to leave Halifax the day after Emma and Mary. He could not trust himself to be with her in a public place and not so much as hold her hand. There would be people at the train station that might know them or their families, especially Charles who was a pillar of the community.

Tonight would be their last time together until something could be arranged in Mahone Bay. Mary had thoughtfully taken her family to a neighbor's for the evening. He waited stretched out on the bed watching the door until Emma quietly entered. They exchanged an electric moment charged with longing and desperation. There was no need for words as she slowly disrobed, revealing a smooth muscular body, long sinewy legs, shapely arms, and milky, rounded breasts erect with anticipation for his touch. His response was quick and urgent. Shedding clothes, he revealed his throbbing desire for the touch of her skin, the melting union that made them one. As she bent over him, her hair swept down like the wings of a dove, her breath sweet and scented like jasmine. Even though his body pulsed for her, he determined to make the loving lengthy, memorable. He kissed her deep and long. Then turning her on her back he began to slowly kiss her face, her neck, her ears, her breasts, down to her very core until she clutched him to her urging "Take me now, my love, I want you NOW!"

Emma and Mary waited on the train platform wrapped in scarves, long woolen coats, broad-brimmed hats, and high leather boots. The bitter north wind found its way in between the trains to bid them farewell, chilling Emma's spirits more deeply. She searched for Andrew, but knew they had agreed he could not come. Mary said it would be best as well. She promised to receive his letters for Emma at the church since she was the one who dealt with mail for the parish.

They boarded the train and settled into the stiff seats as the locomotive's hissing, heavy chug pulled them out of the station. A cloud of white steam burst into the sky. Wearily, Emma surveyed the cold grey of the day from her window. Suddenly, her eye caught a lone figure on the hill waving his hat in wide circles. It was Andrew! She smiled and waved, although likely he could not see her. The vision warmed her smile into a broad grin.

With the train wheels beating a rhythm on the tracks, Emma's eyes closed. Her mind floated on the previous night's sweet memories. The clacking rhythm churned out a tune that comforted.

He promised to write me letters.
He promised to find a way.
He promised to write me letters.
He promised to find a way.

- TWENTY-EIGHT -

Edgar's Welcome

MAHONE BAY, NOVA SCOTIA - JANUARY, 1918

Edgar put on his Sunday-best woolen trousers, vest, and jacket to meet Emma and Mary at Mahone Junction station. A coarse tweed cap pulled over one eye completed the outfit. He would have cut a dashing figure with his tanned skin and bold, dark eyes, if it were not for his long, untrimmed hair and untidy beard. Years at sea did not develop fancy grooming habits, nor did he much care for what he called "the snooty upper class look" like his brother-in-law, with hair all plastered down and parted.

He paced back and forth along the narrow platform muttering curses at the lateness of the train. Charles had ordered him to harness the rectory sleigh to the new mare to bring the women and their belongings, as if he were some kind of servant. Himself being too busy with church meetings. The superior attitude of his brother-in-law always put him in a bad mood.

But things would be changing soon. His prospects were looking up after this last trip to Boston. Arrangements were in place for him to become first mate with a new vessel. They would all change their tune when he came back with pockets full of money. The tea-totaling busybodies would not like how he made it, but bless the prohibitionists for boosting the economy of the fisher folk. Bringing liquor from the Caribbean or Saint Pierre was legal enough, as long as they stayed beyond the twelve-mile limit. Bringing it ashore was another matter, but there was more money in that. He would have to consider taking part in that part of the enterprise, but he was not sure he trusted the men on shore. In any case, he was not going to miss this opportunity to take Emma away and build a home of their own with his profits. She would have to bend to his wishes without the interference of her high and mighty brother and sister-in-law. The next voyage was departing soon so he would have to make the best of his time with his young wife. He couldn't wait to get her alone.

A shrill whistle announced the arrival of the Halifax train. It was two months since he had seen Emma. She should be ready to jump into her husband's waiting arms. As she stepped off the train he was surprised to see an older, weary face. Something was different. Mary looked the same, tight-lipped and glaring at him as if he had just robbed the poor box. The experience in Halifax must have changed Emma. He bent his stocky frame over to kiss her cheek as he took her bags.

"Hello Edgar."

Her voice was lifeless. There was definitely something different. He would wait until they were alone to tell her the good news. "Well my lovely, it's good ta see ya after these long months at sea. I've much ta tell but let's get ya both settled back at the rectory first." The bags were loaded onto the back of the sleigh and the ladies given a warm blanket to protect against the damp chill coming off the ocean.

Edgar cracked the whip at the mare that moved nervously towards an approaching automobile struggling in the slushy snow. He shouted loudly "Git on wi'ya, ya silly beast. That mechanical thing won't eat, ya." A toot from the automobile's horn was interpreted by the young mare as the clang of a racing bell. Lurching forward, they all hung on as the horse set the runners flying towards the shelter of its barn.

At the door Charles greeted each woman with a warm embrace which was out of character from his usual formal greeting. His tall frame bent rigidly over them, and an array of pearly teeth escaped from his neatly-trimmed beard and moustache. His usual somber features crinkled with genuine pleasure.

"I am so very glad to have you both back safe and sound. The bishop's visit came at an inconvenient time. I am very sorry I was unable to meet you at the train station, but you know how things go. I had to attend meeting after meeting, which all seems rather trivial after the experiences you have had in Halifax. I want to hear all about it."

Mary's cheeks glowed looking up at his sparkling smile. "We are extremely glad to be back home, my dear. It has been a dreary, emotional time. Your letters were very welcome letting us know there was some normalcy in the world." She locked her arm in his as they entered the rectory.

Charles paused and turned "Edgar, would you be so good as to take care of the mare and sleigh while we get caught up?"

"Sure thing. Then I've a bit o' catchin' up ta do meself with Emma," he muttered. "You'll see me upstairs soon. Right, me love?"

"Yes, of course. I will come up when you are done."

Charles also picked up the lifeless tone in Emma's voice. "Are you all right? Your face looks as pale as the driven snow."

"Yes, I'm just tired. Nothing to worry about."

"You need to take some time for yourself now, Emma. You always give too much and exhaust yourself."

"There was so much to do. We were all very busy."

"I'll bring your bags up. Get some rest before dinner."

"Thank you, Charles, but you worry about me too much."

Mary gave her a backward, worried glance before entering the house. It would be difficult to keep her secret from Charles. She was torn by two strong loyalties and silently prayed for guidance.

Emma heard Edgar's heavy footsteps on the stair and steeled herself. She had to endure until she could make her escape. He must not suspect her distress. She had endured before. If she closed her eyes she could make herself direct thoughts out of the unpleasant now towards the kind and happy past. She had learned this survival technique when her father died, when the world fell apart. It later sustained her when her marriage proved unhappy.

She would convert Edgar's coarse and lusty advances, his rough bruising thrusts into the gentle caresses of Andrew, whispering his love, sealing promises with passionate kisses. These transformations would be easier now that her mind flowed rich with memories, now that she had hope for a sweeter future.

The next morning Emma escaped the bedroom early to find Mary. She was in the kitchen preparing breakfast, her head full of thoughts about getting caught up on church correspondence and wondering if anyone in the village would be needing her services as a midwife anytime soon.

Emma surprised her with a trembling embrace and an urgent plea, anguish in every word. "Mary you must help me get a letter to Andrew! The most horrible news! Edgar is planning to take me away from here after his next voyage. He's involved with some men in Boston who are in the rum-running trade. They have promised him a fortune. He wants to take me away to Jamaica on his return. We have but a few weeks. I must meet with Andrew to plan our escape soon. Please help me!"

"Oh, my dear! We cannot let this happen." Mary, suddenly short of breath, dropped into a chair with her eyebrows knitted.

Was it time to tell Charles?

"Let me think on it. Write your letter. I will see he gets it."

- TWENTY-NINE -

Planning The Escape

MAHONE BAY, NOVA SCOTIA - FEBRUARY, 1918

Pacing restlessly in the small carriage house behind the rectory, Emma waited for Andrew's arrival. They were risking their first meeting since returning from Halifax, although letters had been exchanged. He promised her he would form a plan for their escape, and she longed to hear it, almost as much as she longed for the warmth and strength of his body next to hers.

They waited seven painful days until Edgar departed on his voyage. His last words still rang in her ears. "Farewell, my pretty. Things will be changin' soon. We'll be off ta the warm, lusty lands of the south with no pious kinfolk ta hinder a man's wishes." She knew all too well what that meant - his cruelty would be unbridled.

A cold chill made her tremble even though she was well protected from the winter air. The soft whinny of the young mare from inside the stable and the crunch of boots in the new-fallen snow brought her to attention. She recognized the vigorous stride.

Andrew cautiously opened the door and whispered, "Emma are you here?"

In the time of two heartbeats she was in his arms. "Oh, how I have missed you!"

"And I you, my love." His eyes closed as he bent to kiss her forehead, her cheek, her upturned lips. Squeezing her gently in his arms he whispered, "I want to be with you now and forever. I have found a way."

With flushed cheeks, she pulled back to look into his face. "How I have longed to hear it! Tell me."

"A friend of mine has a place in Newfoundland, a small farm just outside of Trinity Bay. The farm has been abandoned since his grandmother died last year, and he has no use for it. He is a sea captain who will be sailing to St. John's once the weather improves. He can take us there to start a new life."

Emma threw her arms around Andrew her heart dancing in a joyful rhythm. Suddenly she pulled back, her face overcast. "But what of your mother and the farm here? You cannot leave her on her own."

"It is so like you to think of her, dear Emma. We have just heard that my brother, Robert, will be returning from the war. He has sustained some injuries but is well. He will be arriving in Halifax soon. It is all falling into place. You must prepare yourself to leave within the next few weeks."

The embrace that followed swept them into their own world of endless possibilities. The dream that would soon become a reality uplifted them both into a passion that flowed like liquid through their veins. The cool air and the urgency of their need did not allow for total disrobement, but within a moment they were lying on the soft straw with limbs entwined and mouths fully engaged, oblivious to all the world outside.

Emma spent the next weeks in stealthy preparation and secret meetings with Andrew. She felt she had to confide in Mary who helped her to rapidly exchange letters and diverted Charles' attention from her frequent absences. Charles would have to be told before she left, difficult as that might be.

Mary was distraught about Emma's forthcoming departure fearing what Edgar's reaction would be. "You must take the utmost caution. Tell no one exactly where you will be, not even Charles and me. Then, we will not be forced to tell falsehoods, and he cannot read it in our faces."

Emma tried to sooth her fears, even though they haunted her own mind constantly. Although she knew it was dangerous, she could not part with all of Andrew's letters. She kept some hidden in an opening in the closet wall, and stole secret moments alone to read them over and over. They bolstered her courage, keeping her spirits high.

Mary kept her occupied with projects in the parish. Charles organized workers to get more assistance for the homeless in Halifax while Mary spearheaded the church auxiliary efforts to knit gloves, socks and scarves for the homeless, as well as the troops in the war. Amongst the busy clatter of knitting needles and food drives, Emma's mind was elsewhere. She knew that Edgar would be back from his voyage in a few short weeks. Her meetings with Andrew and the anticipation of Robert's return which would allow their final escape, were her focus as the dreary winter days dragged by.

- THIRTY -

LAURA MAKES DECISIONS

HALIFAX, NOVA SCOTIA – DECEMBER 22, 1985

With the highway winding in front of her, bordered by the hoar-frosted forest glittering in the sunlight, Laura drove as if on automatic pilot. The surrounding beauty of wintry hillsides flashed by unseen.

The last few nights had been restless, disturbed by Emma's constant presence. It was as if she were reliving her affair with Andrew through Laura. Tossing in her bed, heated by erotic pleasures, then chilled by an unrelenting fear, Laura found writing to be her only release. She often rose from her unrest to write far into the night.

Now her mind buzzed with questions and doubts. Was her current decision to stay at Ray's house tonight a result of her immersion in Emma's love story? Or was she interjecting her own longing for Ray in her writing? No, Emma's visits left no doubt about the passion experienced with Andrew. But was there also a message for Laura? If so, why now?

With a start, she realized she was approaching

Halifax and must decide which turnoff to take to get to Doc MacKinnon's office in Bedford. It was late in the day. Hopefully, she would not have to wait too long. As it turned out, there was no one in the waiting room. She was shown into his office right away.

Doc MacKinnon's practiced smile turned into a glow when she walked in wearing a black sheath dress that accentuated every curve. "I'm glad to see you again, Laura. You're looking so much better today, in fact, exceptionally lovely."

"Thank you. I'm heading to a party at Ray's this evening."

"I wanted to schedule you at the end of the day so we could have a visit. I received your x-rays yesterday, and there is an area of concern we have to discuss." He pulled out the x-ray photo from the envelop on his desk and pointed to her abdominal region. "Now, I don't want to alarm you unduly but this dark area here indicates a growth of some kind. It appears to be in the uterus. It could be entirely benign, but we need to take a look at it. Sooner, rather than later would be the best course. Since you are one of my special patients and I have some pull," he said with a wink, "I've booked you with a gynecologist who can see you Monday to schedule an operation."

Laura stared at the x-ray, her face frozen with disbelief. This was the last thing she expected.

The accident seemed so trivial, just a bump. Now this! It must be serious. An appointment with a specialist isn't ar-

ranged so quickly!

Doc MacKinnon read her fears and patted her tensed hand. "Now, it's likely nothing to worry about, but we do have to take precautions. I have to ask if there is any chance you might be pregnant."

"No, I've just had my period."

"Good. That would have complicated the situation. Try not to stress. Dr. Jamieson will get this done as quickly as possible. Have a relaxing weekend, and give my best to Ray."

She was still trying to process his words. "Thank you. This was so unexpected. You have been very helpful and thorough."

"This accident could be a life saver," she thought as she left the office in a daze.

Ray would be waiting for her at his house. There was so much to tell him. When she arrived, the caterers were just leaving. Of course, the party! People would be arriving soon. There was little time to ask Ray about waiting to accept the award. Now there were two valid reasons for a delay.

Was she confident enough in their relationship to tell him about Emma? Would he think she was crazy?

Perhaps the revelation about that reason should wait. She would have to feel this out carefully. She could not afford to lose his support right now.

He greeted her at the door with a smile that lit up his face and glowing eyes that never left hers. He gave her a gentle hug that lingered. "I'm so glad you came. How are you doing? What did Doc MacKinnon have to say? I've been worried about you."

"Well, I do have some news."

"Come in out of the cold and I'll get something to warm you up." He took her coat while she sat in the living room and admired the Christmas decorations, all gold and sparkling from tree top to mantle. He returned shortly and sat next to her with two hot rum toddies.

"Okay, I've waited long enough. What's up?"

"It's an unwelcome surprise but it looks like I'm in for some surgery next week. The x-ray showed a growth in my uterus which may or may not be something to worry about."

He drew her closer. "Laura, I'm so sorry. I know the Doc. He'll see that you get the best treatment as soon as possible. I don't know much about these problems, but I understand that many growths are benign. Even if they're not, early treatment is very successful."

"I guess I'm a little shaken by it all. I'm thinking that I should wait a semester before accepting the award to continue on with my thesis."

He put his arm around her and kissed her cheek. "Whatever you think is best. That shouldn't be a problem."

She hesitated, looking into his eyes for reassurance. "There's also a writing project I need to complete. I'd like to tell you about it."

Just then the doorbell rang and loud voices started a

chorus of "We Wish You a Merry Christmas".

"It can wait till later."

"Of course. I want to give it my undivided attention."

The party seemed to last forever. She was in no frame of mind to interact with her younger, fellow graduate students. Conversations were silly and trivial tinged with too much rum punch. The profs attending droned on about their various projects. The punch numbed her a little which made it more bearable. She didn't want to make her relationship with Ray a topic of gossip, so kept a polite distance from him, all the while feeling his eyes searching her out. It was difficult to hide what she wanted most - the comfort of his warm embrace. Finally, the last of the guests were departing. In a loud voice, she offered to help Ray clean up.

As soon as the door closed Ray was at her side holding a sprig of mistletoe above their heads. His kiss was long. Sensual flicks of his tongue sent flashes of white light coursing through her. Muscular thighs pressed into her, and there was no doubt that his desire was as strong as hers. He escorted her up the stairs to the bedroom, closed the door and pressed her against it with a throbbing need she shared. Their lips and tongues touched gently at first, then deeply, urgently. Clothing fell around them, allowing skin-to-skin shock waves to engulf them. He pressed eager lips to her neck, her pulsing breast, then gently wrapped his mouth around an erect nipple.

Her back arched bringing them even closer. The electric spell of his entry ignited every part of her. She became lost in sensuous exploration, new and exciting, ending in a long, lustful dance that exhausted them both. Everything else could wait until morning.

Laura awoke to the crackling of the fireplace and the distant sounds of dishes rattling in the kitchen. The alarm clock was silent but notified her that she had slept late. She stretched, enjoying a feeling of wellbeing. This was the first good sleep she could remember since finding the journal. She rose to go to the bathroom, and when she returned Ray was sitting on the bed with a tray of coffee and sweets left over from the party.

"Good morning gorgeous. I thought you might need something to keep up your strength and sustain your beautiful body."

"My body thanks you in more ways than one. The coffee smells wonderful."

"I made it myself. I can be quite handy you know."

"I noticed." They shared a smile as he squeezed her hand between his soft palms, then pressed it to his lips.

"I have an overwhelming impulse to jump back into bed with you, but I need you to be fully charged with caffeine and talk to me about a couple of things. First of all, have you heard from your husband?"

This is the last thing she wanted to talk about. "No. Although I don't really care about my marriage anymore,

I would like to know where the hell he is. His office called looking for him the other day. It's not like him not to report to work. I guess I'll have to call them Monday to see if Ted showed up. But let's not talk about him. What I can tell you is that I've made up my mind that it's over. Right now, all I can deal with is one problem at a time."

"I can understand why you've made that decision. I'm selfishly happy, but know it can't be easy. We'll manage your problems together starting with your doctor's appointment. My main concern is your health. But I need to know about this writing project. You've been hard to get hold of lately, so I know it must be important."

These were all words she wanted to hear. "You're going to think I've lost my mind."

"If you've lost it, I'll help you find it." He said hugging her and kissing her forehead.

The tension around her jaw eased off. "First, I have to ask - do you believe in ghosts?"

Ray began to laugh, but then he saw that she wasn't joking. "If you're serious, I have to remind you that I'm a native of the Maritimes with a strong Welsh heritage. All my life I've heard stories that can't be explained, real stories from sources I trust. In fact, one of my relations lives in the old hydra stone buildings that they built following the Halifax explosion. He claims that several times he has seen the ghost of a sea captain climbing the stairs looking lost. This from a man who has an administrative position at Dalhousie University. I could tell you many such stories. They weren't all just spinning yarns."

"Well then, be prepared to hear another one." Laura locked his eyes to decipher his expression. "Emma, my great-grandmother has become part of my life. She visits me constantly. Although I know she's not a danger, she'll not leave me alone until I've written her story."

Ray showed no sign of disbelief, only intense interest. "Good God girl! No wonder I haven't heard from you lately. Start from the beginning. I want to know everything."

- THIRTY-ONE -

MISSING

HALIFAX, NOVA SCOTIA - DECEMBER, 1985

Laura stayed with Ray until Monday. On her drive back to Mahone Bay she reflected on how this man was changing her life. He was an oasis of calm, so easy to be with, so understanding. She felt comfortable discussing anything with him without feeling foolish, especially her bizarre relationship with Emma. For the first time, in a very long time, the man she was with was there to support her, not to question and direct her every move.

Her doctor's appointment with the gynecologist went as Doc McKinnon had predicted. The surgery was scheduled for the end of the week. There was no point in worrying until the results of the biopsy gave them some answers.

She would continue her writing until then. The fact that Ray said he would be available to assist her efforts gave her a surge of energy. He could help her with the historical background being very familiar with the difficulties of that period. Best of all, he would be her sounding board when she was not sure about her assumptions. When the time came for her operation, he would be there to help with whatever followed. Despite the dreary grey skies and rain that was washing away all the beautiful snow, she felt uplifted. Like that journey of a thousand miles, she now felt confident to handle things one step at a time.

At Mahone Bay, her first step was towards the blinking light of the answering machine. She was expecting Ted's voice but this voice was more pleasing to her ear.

"It's Aunt Rosie. Where've ya been….er…I mean I knows where, but what's happenin'? You know, between you and that new feller…er…I mean…er…is he good? No. I mean do ya like him or what? I hates these damn machines. Call me."

Laura had to laugh. Ted could wait. Rosie always wanted to know all. Her call back received no answer. Then, she remembered that Rosie spent Mondays with her quilting group. She'd talk with her later.

She pressed the recorder for the last message. It was not Ted's voice but had the same tone of irritation.

"Hello. It's Monday and this is Dean at the office. Ted, are you there? We are really concerned. You have missed the last two meetings and your clients are not happy. Can someone call us back please?"

This was not like Ted. Work was everything. An upset boss calling would have him spinning. Not even sexual meanderings would come before his drive for success.

Something was definitely wrong!

Laura dialed the office and tried to keep her voice steady. "Hello, Dean. This is Laura McGinty. I haven't heard from Ted for over a week. We've been having our difficulties, but it's not like him to miss work. I think I'll have to make a police report. I'm afraid he's had an accident or gone missing for some reason."

"Okay, Laura. Thanks for letting us know. I'm sure there's some good reason, but filing a report is a good idea. The police will have the resources to check it out."

"I'm going to phone the hospitals first. I'll get back to you when I know anything."

The hospital calls drew a blank. Before contacting the police, she tried to remember details of the last time she saw Ted. He had come home drunk. She had locked him out of the bedroom and went back to sleep. Then she heard terrible shouting as he came running out of the spare bedroom yelling something about this bloody house with its freaking ghost. He was in such a hurry that he didn't even grab his coat. She thought at the time that he finally saw Emma and would now believe her. But why was he in such a panic?

He should not have been driving.

A cold draft made her shiver as she wondered about Emma's part in this. Perhaps she wasn't as benign as Rosie had thought. Did she have some sort of antagonism towards Ted? There WERE similarities between Ted and Edgar.

She needed to speak to Ray and took a deep breath as she reached for the phone. This was going to sound crazy.

She felt better after their conversation. He had calmed her down in his usual way, applying logic to the problem. It made sense. He advised her to be careful about what she told the police as they normally don't take ghost threats seriously. In any case, there was no proof that the ghost had anything to do with Ted's disappearance. He might be off on a bender with his girlfriend as she had originally thought. All the police needed to know was that Ted left the house in the middle of the night in an angry, drunken state when she locked him out of the bedroom.

Laura returned from the police station and paced the floor restlessly. She called Ray again.

"It's as if they think I have something to do with his disappearance. I feel like I've been put through a meat grinder, all bits and pieces."

"Try not to stress. I know that's like saying try not to breathe, but there's nothing you can do now except wait."

"That's not my strong suit."

"I think you should continue with your writing including some of the historical bits I suggested. It will take your mind off Ted. I'd say come here, but it's probably best if you stay near the phone right now. I'm sure there'll be some news soon. Let me know. I'll come by Thursday as soon as my classes are over to pick you up. We'll deal with that surgery together."

"Thanks Ray. I don't know what I'd do without you."

"Don't even think about trying."

She liked the way his voice smiled when he said the words.

Before sitting at her typewriter, she had to call Rosie to bring her up to date. Otherwise, she would be in for a lot of scolding and unwanted interruptions. The story writing must go on. She was more sure of it than ever. The reasons why Emma was directing her actions would be revealed in time…she hoped.

- THIRTY-TWO -

Conscription

MAHONE BAY, NOVA SCOTIA – APRIL, 1918

Charles sought the solitude of his study to take his morning tea and gather his thoughts before the tasks of the day descended. This was his quiet time in the room filled with his books, his photographs, and the diaries of his work in the parish.

He opened the newspaper to get the latest reports. Things are not going well for the allies. Additional troops were being sent, newly conscripted by the law imposed last August by Prime Minister Borden. There had been heated debates and protests at the time.

The Quebecers were in opposition of course. No love for the British there, he thought bitterly. Do they not know we are all in this together! Battles are being lost for lack of troops. Still, it meant more young men would be leaving while workers were needed here so desperately. He scanned the list of new conscripts that he acquired from the local council and sighed deeply, setting it aside.

Much of his time was spent consoling grieving families, not only for the soldiers lost in the battlefields, but for the victims lost in the disastrous explosion in Halifax. He turned to the latest estimates in the newspaper article: approximately two thousand dead, nine thousand wounded, sixteen hundred buildings destroyed with another twelve thousand damaged! Property damage is thought to be over thirty-five million dollars. No wonder it is being called the largest man-made explosion in history.

It is impossible to say exactly how many died, since some people were literally blown to bits. Information from the shell-shocked survivors is still being gathered. Some will never have the answers they seek. A hundred and twenty-four of the unidentified bodies were buried in a mass grave at Potter's Field on Bayer's Road.

It was certainly the darkest day Halifax has ever seen. To add to the misfortune, when the munitions ship blew up in the harbor, the hospitals had been full of wounded soldiers brought from the battlefields. How ironic that one of the greatest Canadian losses of the war should happen right at home, caused by the collision of two allied ships.

How many more could have been rescued but for the horrendous blizzard that blew in the next two days, followed by rain and more freezing? God's will can be hard to bear and understand sometimes. The events of the times tested the faith of many in his congregation.

Instead of the price gouging and looting that followed the disaster, Charles tried to focus on the goodwill that sprang from the hearts of men at this time of great need. That hospital train sent from Boston the next day by the governor of Massachusetts would never be forgotten. Food and fundraising drives were still happening across the province, the rest of Canada, and other parts of the world, to aid the homeless, the injured, and the orphaned. As the weather eased and building supplies could be brought in, the rebuilding process had begun with the help of many hands.

Mobilizing the depleting resources of his community to give aid took whatever spare time was left in his daily schedule. The spiritual and emotional needs of his parishioners drained all his energy. Never was he so taxed as a minister.

Emma was usually an enthusiastic assistant but seemed so distant and melancholy since her return from Halifax. Such sad times! Small wonder it has affected her so.

Of course, that husband of hers makes her life a misery, drunken lout that he is. He would never forgive himself, as her custodian, for agreeing to their marriage. The charlatan turned like Jekyll and Hyde when it suited him.

Charles recalled the evening when he returned to the rectory to hear Edgar's voice booming from the upper hallway. Mary was at the bottom of the stairs wide-eyed, wringing her hands.

"Wretched woman! Do you think yourself a wife, gone for weeks, wandering the streets of Halifax like a common slattern! No decent woman walks about the town at night. My own mates were there and saw ya, so don't deny it," he slurred.

"Edgar. I was running errands for the hospital. There was no one else available to choose what was needed."

"Lying slut! There were soldiers following you."

A loud slap resounded as Emma shrieked in terror. "No, please. They were coming to help me carry the supplies."

He saw Edgar lunge after her as she ran to the bedroom and locked the door behind her. Edgar's loud curses and pounding at the door followed.

He was frozen with indecision not wanting to interfere in marital problems yet angered by the brute.

Mary tugged at his coat sleeves. "Charles, for God's sake do something!"

It was all he needed. He bounded up the stairs and blocked the access to the bedroom. "Good heavens, man! Get hold of yourself. Leave the woman alone until you are of sober mind. Do you really think that badly of her?"

Edgar's upper lip curled and spittle sprayed as he spoke. "She's not doin' her wifely duties. It's me she should be ministering to, not the low life of Halifax. You lot are such do-gooders. Ya think yer better than the rest of us. But she's MY wife an' needs ta do MY biddin'." He shook his fist as he spoke looking like a thundercloud firing out its lightening.

Charles would not be bullied. He had straightened to his imposing six feet and glared back at the swarthy man undaunted. "As long as you are living here, Edgar, you must abide by MY rules. There will be no more drunken brutality."

"Yeah, well, we'll see about that. Things'll be changin' after this voyage."

Plodding down the stairs with heavy footsteps, Edgar exited in a funk, slamming the door so forcefully that Mary's fine china rattled in the dining room.

Charles remembered the smell of rum as Edgar pushed by him. He continued to wonder about this mysterious voyage that would change everything. Too many of the seafaring folk had been tempted into the rum running trade. Times were hard and the money they could earn was good. His sermons on the morality of the situation appeared to do little good.

At least he is gone for the time being. Emma had been glad to see him go and can rest easy for a while yet.

I will have to find a way to keep him in line.

A timid knock interrupted the sour recollections of that night. Emma peeked around the heavy oak door. Charles was surprised that she should suddenly appear just as he was thinking of her situation.

"Sorry to disturb you, Charles. I was wondering if you have a few moments."

"Always for you, dear sister." He noticed her normally fair complexion was now shockingly pale. "What is the matter?"

She raised her eyes to Charles and squared her shoulders. "There's something I must discuss with you." She hesitated, then continued in short bursts.

"Have you heard that Robert Burgess has returned from the war? He has lost an arm. He's in a very confused state of mind. I know his brother Andrew."

"Yes, another cruel casualty. It's dreadful." Charles surveyed the list on his desk. His eyebrows formed arrows of disbelief. "I thought I saw a Burgess here. It's inconceivable! The government has chosen this time to conscript Andrew."

Emma turned to the window to hide her face. Her voice was barely audible. "No! It cannot be true."

"I'm afraid so Emma. Do you know the family well?" He glanced up and was startled to see her sink into a chair as if the floor had disappeared beneath her feet. "Emma, are you all right?"

"I…oh, I feel a bit weak, lack of sleep, perhaps. I keep having these dizzy spells." She bent over slightly and took a few deep breaths. Charles came to her side and moved to take her hand. She grasped his tightly instead.

"But, Charles, can't you do something about Andrew's conscription? He will be needed here."

"I will write a letter today, but do not hold out much hope. I have had little success in the past. But really,

Emma, you must take better care of yourself. You have been working much too hard."

"As have you, dear brother. We must do what we can. I think I will walk out to the orchard to take some air. It always lifts my spirits."

"Do not over-exert yourself. And dress warmly. There is a cool breeze coming off the water."

"Yes, I will take care."

Emma closed the door behind her, then climbed the stairs as rapidly as she could. In the privacy of her room she quickly wrote a note to Andrew and sealed it. She would place it in their meeting place in the orchard. He would check there before returning home after market today.

They must meet tonight!

- THIRTY-THREE -

THE ORCHARD

MAHONE BAY, NOVA SCOTIA - APRIL, 1918

Andrew paced back and forth beside the ancient apple tree to keep warm in the damp April air. Tethered to its trunk, his horse breathed heavily exhaling steamy mists as it bent its neck to nibble on new greens. In the cool moonlight, its ebony coat glistened with the recent exertion. Its master's impatient urgings could not be ignored. Andrew stopped to stroke the horse's neck, took a cloth from his saddlebag, and wiped down its flanks to prevent the chill from settling in.

A chorus of frogs from the nearby pond filled the night with their primal mating song, a magical harmonious sound vibrating the air with the essence of regeneration. Andrew listened intently, but his mind was tuned more closely for another sound, the sound of footsteps. He repeatedly searched the orchard path leading from the rectory.

She should have been here by now.

A dozen fears raced through his head accompanied

by a longing, over which he had no control. In a few short months, this bewitching woman with bold blue eyes and silken skin had turned his life upside down and sideways.

Yet he recalled it was her courage and compassion that first drew him to her during the terrible aftermath of the explosion. Emma reached out to all, bearing the weight of human sorrow with the strength of an eagle and the gentleness of a dove.

The memory of that first embrace when her body clung to his was bittersweet. To pursue her after she confessed that she was married was madness, but it was soon clear that Emma's unfortunate marriage trapped her in a loveless prison. Mary's warnings of Edgar's violent nature only strengthened his desire to save her.

Andrew's thoughts were interrupted by the glimmer of a lantern winding through the trees. His feet raced towards the light in step with his heartbeats. When he reached the hooded figure, his strong arms enfolded her body, overwhelming the chill with the heat of a deep and fervent kiss. They turned up the path with arms entwined seeking the old apple tree whose sheltering limbs gave them refuge from the outside world.

"What took you so long, my love? I have lived a lifetime of worry."

"I could not let Charles see me leave. I had to wait until he went up to his room. Oh, Andrew, what are we going to do? Charles told me you have been conscripted. If you leave for the war, all our plans will be for naught.

Charles is writing a letter to request an abstention but is not hopeful. We must act before Edgar returns."

He sensed she was teetering on the edge of tears and drew her closer, stroking her back as he spoke, keeping his voice calm to ease her anxiety. "We will work it out Emma. The most important thing is to get you away from Edgar. Can you be ready by tomorrow evening? I have told my mother and brother that you will be coming. All is well. They are eager to meet you. Do not fret, my love."

"I will be more than ready, but what can I tell Charles? He will be so disappointed in me."

"You will find a way, and he will bear it because he loves you. But take care. No one must know where you are, else Edgar hears of it, not even Mary."

"Mary is my dearest friend. I have told her our plans, but she did not want to know exactly where I will be so she would not have to lie to Edgar. I know she will keep our secret."

He observed the pain in her face and nodded in agreement, even though there was doubt in his mind. He wanted to protect her, to keep her safe, a feeling that nearly equaled his desire. Spreading his coat beneath the branches, he drew her down and turned the lantern off.

"Lay with me, my love. We must make the best of our time together. It may be short."

As the moonlight filtered through the budding branches, Emma knelt. She removed her cape to release dark curls falling over a thin nightdress that barely covered her ample breasts, nipples now erect in the cool night air. Aroused and waiting, Andrew took her face gently in his hands. Their mouths joined in a growing passion, flaming like an inferno. As she reclined, he bent over to undo her bodice. He kissed her exposed skin sending them both into a frenzy of shedding garments. Her body opened to him like a flower to the morning sun, blossoming fully in the rising heat of their passion. His flesh melted into hers. Throbbing to the same beat as the primordial chorus whose fervor echoed around them, they became one.

- THIRTY-FOUR -

Emma's Goodbyes

MAHONE BAY, NOVA SCOTIA - APRIL, 1918

Emma rose early the next morning and quietly began packing the things she could not leave behind: her mother's locket containing pictures of both parents, her grandmother's silk shawl, her Sunday bonnet, a small assortment of her best clothes, combs and toiletries that were hard to replace, the wood carving of a horse Charles had made for her when she was a child.

What could she tell him? There could be no lies between them. He had taken over as her parent when their mother and father died, her mother of scarlet fever in 1913 and her father lost in a shipwreck shortly after. She was a girl of fifteen and Charles thirteen years older, already in the ministry. He thought it best for her to go to boarding school in Halifax but corresponded and saw her often. He was her role model, her mentor, her friend.

She could not bear to see his disappointment. Kind as he was, he would not understand the passion that drove her to abandon her sacred marriage vows. She picked up the pen and slowly scribed reasons she hoped he and Mary could accept.

Dearest Charles and Mary,

I think you know of my unhappiness with Edgar. I live in constant fear that he will take me away from all I hold dear to some faraway land. I also fear he will spread his venom to you in some vile fit of temper. He is a danger to us all. I must escape and now is the perfect time.

Do not worry about me. I have found a protector, but can tell you no more for all our sakes. In time, I hope that circumstances will change, and I can return to your good graces. I will let you know more when I can.

Please forgive me for not being the perfect sister you deserve. I love you both very much.

Your devoted,
Emma

Mary was the more tolerant of the two and her dearest friend. She could not leave without saying goodbye to her. She would understand. Emma heard Charles rush out the front door to meet with the parish council. He would be gone most of the day. She made her way to the kitchen. Mary sat eating dry biscuits with her tea and when she approached, gave her a dazzling smile.

"You have come down at last. I have exciting news. For

these past months, I have suffered with weariness, nausea, and dizziness. My suspicions have been confirmed by the doctor. We are going to have a baby. After all these years of trying I can hardly believe it." Her face glowed with joy and thanksgiving like a cherub on a chapel wall.

Emma rushed to throw her arms around her. "Oh, Mary, that is wonderful news! You have helped so many babes into the world. At last, you will be the one receiving. I could not be happier for you and Charles."

"Of course, I want you to assist at the birth and be the godmother."

Emma's face dropped into sadness as she pulled away.

"What's wrong? Does that not please you?"

"It makes my news harder to tell. I am leaving tonight Mary. I must go before Edgar returns. You know that he plans to take me away when the voyage is done."

The joy suddenly left Mary's face. Tears swelled into the corners of her eyes. "But how will you manage?"

"Andrew will be coming for me tonight. We will go to his farm until we can make our way to Newfoundland." She hesitated, then continued with an urgency in her voice. "There is a complication. Charles just told me that Andrew has been conscripted. I know he will go if Charles cannot obtain an abstention for him. If he is drawn into the war, I will stay with his mother and brother until his return. But, Mary, you must swear not to tell anyone about us, not even Charles. If Edgar hears of it, all will be lost."

Mary lowered her eyes to her lap and clasped her hands as if in prayer. With downturned mouth, she slowly replied. "Yes, I will swear, but are you very sure this is what you want? Your plan is full of danger, and Charles will be distraught without you, as will I."

"You know I will miss you both terribly, but Andrew has come into my life like a guardian angel. We love each other very much and trust in that love to see us through this. I promise you that if there is any way, I will come back when your baby is due."

Mary rose to embrace Emma. They lingered as tears began to fall. Pulling away gently, Emma continued in a quavering voice. "I must get my belongings into the coach house before Charles returns. We will leave late tonight. I have left a note for the both of you, but please do not let on that you know more."

"You can count on me, but do try to let me know how you are doing. I could not bear the worry without hearing from you."

Emma forced a smile. "I will. In the meantime, dear friend, we will have one more day together."

As Emma hurried away to finish her packing her stomach churned, and a sour taste rose to her mouth. Mary's symptoms were all too familiar. She blanched at the possibility, emotions swirling in a circle between fear and joy. It could only be Andrew's child. However joyful, a pregnancy would bring another complication, making her escape even more urgent. She would wait until she was sure before telling Mary. Distracted by these thoughts, it was the next day before she remembered that Andrew's letters had been left in the closet wall.

- THIRTY-FIVE -

Recovery

MAHONE BAY, NOVA SCOTIA – DECEMBER, 1985

Somehow the week quickly slipped by and Laura felt pleased with the progress of her writing. Emma must have been pleased as well, since she left her alone for the most part - except for the one night, the night Laura had the vision of the mystical orchard where Emma and Andrew made love. She woke in a sweat with the sound of the amphibian chorus throbbing in her ears. Surrounded by an aura of luminescent blue, Emma stood at the foot of Laura's bed with a puzzling countenance, simultaneously joyful and sad. Everything Laura had learned about Emma's story showed in the ghostly face at that moment. Laura's hand reached out to her in total empathy, joining thoughts as the eerie blue turned to white and disappeared.

But now, it was time to put thoughts of Emma aside and enter the reality of her life. Ray was coming in an hour to pick her up. She had to pack a few things as he wanted her to stay for the weekend after the operation.

She would have to notify the police that she would be in Halifax for the next few days and give them Ray's number.

There was still no word from Ted. She should be more concerned, but her anger against him was strong; stronger still was her curiosity.

Where the hell was he!

Without a tinge of guilt, she packed her most alluring negligee. She looked forward to one more night with Ray before she faced the scalpel.

Laura's eyelids fluttered open fighting against the harsh lights of the recovery room. Her vision blurred, then focused on the smiling nurse looking down on her.

"The sleeping beauty's coming around." She took Laura's wrist and checked her pulse. "You're doing just great. There's this good-looking, princely type waiting for you, lucky girl. He can come visit till the doctor's ready to see you."

Ray's face peeked around the curtain with a broad grin. "You're back and still looking gorgeous."

Laura lifted her free hand to pull some straggling hairs behind her ear. "Yes, I just bet I am. Did you happen to see that bus that ran me over?"

"You'll be fine in no time, but I must insist. No jogging for a day."

"Very funny. Right now, I think the walk to the car will be a challenge."

"You forget to whom you are speaking, missy. These

bulging muscles can carry you wherever you would like to go."

"How about some nice tropical island?"

"Hmmm. I'll have to give that some thought."

The door pushed open, and Laura's gynecologist briskly opened the curtain.

"Oh, excuse me, Mr. and Mrs. McGinty. I just wanted to have a few words. How are you feeling?"

"Groggy and sore."

"That will ease up in a little while. Everything went well. We were able to remove the growth cleanly. It's a good thing you weren't pregnant. It was the size of a large orange and could have caused a baby some problems. I want you to make an appointment at the end of next week when we'll have the biopsy report. It's still too early to tell if you'll need any more treatment. Right now, I just want you to rest for a couple of hours. If vital signs are good you can go home."

"Thank you doctor. Is there anything I need to be careful of?

"No extreme exercise for the next week. You can resume normal marital relations when your body tells you it's okay. I'll see you next week." With a quick wave he was out the door and down the hall to the next patient.

With the color already flushing her cheeks, Laura watched Ray intently to scan his reaction. "Sorry, I didn't feel like going into a discussion about you not being my husband and about him being missing."

There was reassurance in his calming smile. "No need to think about Ted right now. Rest is what the doctor ordered, and I'm going to make sure you get it."

"The nurse was right. You are prince-like."

"All right then, princess. We'll be getting you to the castle before the day is out."

When they got to Ray's house he tucked her into a comfy feather quilt and made her some hot chocolate. "You get some rest now. We can talk some more about your writing project tomorrow. From what I've read so far, I think there'll be many who want to hear Emma's story."

"Ray I've been thinking a lot about Emma's visits with me. What stands out now is that when Ted was pushing to start a family, she warned me not to have a baby now. She was right for so many reasons. The last part of her story is terribly sad, but I'm thinking I must have learned about it for a reason."

"It sounds like she's your guardian angel. After all, you are her only direct descendant. You'll figure it out. Now's the time to sleep and get stronger. Your prince has spoken." He kissed her forehead and brought the covers up to her chin.

She sighed as her eyelids drooped. "Yes, I like that…. my guardian angel."

By the time she returned to Mahone Bay Laura felt pampered, rested, and eager to work on Emma's story. At the very least, it would take her mind off the biopsy results. Liking their new roles as collaborators in the project, she could not wait to show Ray the next new twist in Emma's unfolding drama.

- THIRTY-SIX -

THE BURGESS FARM

LUNENBURG COUNTY, NOVA SCOTIA - APRIL 1918

As the buggy pulled into the long laneway bordered by a lofty mix of deciduous and evergreen growth, Emma gazed up at a full moon that shone like a beacon to her new home. She took it as a good omen. She was pleased to see a charming, gothic-styled farmhouse with three gables on the second story and a roofed porch around the front. It faced the ocean situated on a grassy hill. From far below, the surf could be heard pounding against a craggy cliff. Behind the house a red barn bordered by a fenced enclosure faced acres of fields ready for planting. She leaned a weary head on Andrew's shoulder wondering whether this was a dream.

Although the hour was late, two figures appeared at the entrance, both lean and tall like Andrew. As the buggy drew nearer, the resemblance was more acute featuring the same light blue eyes and square chin; although the man had a thick, blonde moustache and shaggy, long hair, and the woman's stern face was etched with weathered lines. She grabbed a knitted shawl to wrap around her braided crown of graying hair as they walked towards the new arrivals.

Andrew helped Emma down and presented her to his mother, Louisa, and brother Robert. "This is my precious Emma. I hope you will learn to love her as I do."

His Mother spoke with a slight German accent. Her broad youthful smile dispelled all signs of age and severity. "Welcome my child. We have been waiting to meet you. Andrew was right. You are as pretty as a bouquet of spring flowers. Such a sweet face. Come, you must be tired. Andrew take her things upstairs. Robert will take the buggy to the barn."

Robert nodded and smiled shyly at Emma.

"Thank you Mrs. Burgess. You are making me feel most welcome."

"You are family now. Please, call me Louisa."

As Robert approached the barn door, two large German shepherd dogs greeted him with a chorus of barking. They spun in youthful excitement as he opened the door, then sniffing a new scent bounded off towards Emma. Robert whistled a command and came running after them. They stopped to wait for him, with alert ears, then followed behind as he came up to Emma. He spoke to them in German and they sat down. "These two ruffians are called Hans and Helga. They will not hurt you once they know you are family."

Emma bent over smiling and put her hand out so the

dogs could take in her scent. They sniffed, whined, and eventually competed to lick her hand. "They are beautiful! I think we will be good friends, Robert. Don't worry. I like dogs."

Louisa gave a hearty laugh. "Yah. Once they figure that out, you won't be able to get rid of them. Come. Let us go inside. It is cold." With her arm around Emma's waist she escorted her up the path to the waiting warmth of the house.

In a month's time Emma wrote an urgent letter to Mary.

May 20, 1918

Dearest Mary,

I am daring to send this letter to the rectory knowing that you open the mail. I hope that your pregnancy is going well. I think of you and Charles daily. I am enjoying life on the farm even though the workday is long and hard. Being with Andrew makes every chore seem easy. I was glad to provide extra help in the busy days of spring planting and have even learned new skills like milking the cows and churning butter. It appears I am not a city girl after all.

His family has been very kind. Louisa Burgess is a warm, loving woman. I can see where Andrew gets his good nature. Robert, his brother, is a kind but troubled soul. He will not talk of the war and the loss of his arm. He is often found on his own, quiet and brooding. At times, he wakes the household with his nightmares which makes me very afraid for my Andrew.

He has learned that he must report for military duty in Halifax at the end of the month. The request for abstention has been denied. I have tried to persuade him to run off to Newfoundland with me, but he refuses to break the law and put me at risk of being stranded there without him if he is caught. He also does not want any accusations regarding his German heritage, even though his great grandfather Zwicker first settled in Nova Scotia in the mid 1700's.

He tries to assure me that the war will end soon, and we will then start our new life. He feels I will be well protected with Robert in charge at the farm, but it all gives me an uneasy feeling.

I am writing not only to share my grieving for his departure, but also to ask whether you have heard anything from Edgar. I know he must be back now and live in fear that he will find me. It is unfair of me to share such anxiety when you are in a delicate state, but please write soon with any news. You can send it in care of Louisa Burgess at the post office in Lunenburg.

Your ever affectionate,
Emma

When Mary received the letter she hastily tore open the envelope. It was necessary to respond immediately with a warning.

May 25, 1918

Dearest Emma,

I was so relieved to get your letter although your news is not as good as we had hoped. My daily prayers that all the madness in Europe will end soon will also include prayers for Andrew's safety. You must remain strong while he is away.

We are both well. I am glad to have the nausea part of my pregnancy over. At the moment, I am blessed with good energy and am definitely eating for two! Of course, Charles fusses much too much and will not let me do anything that might tire me.

As for Edgar, I am sorry to report that he is indeed back from his voyage and was in a rage when he found you had left. Thank God Charles was here to confront him, as he did not believe us when we said we did not know where you had gone. Charles went so far as to show him your letter. Charles then demanded that he gather his things and leave. I can still see the distorted features of his face and his final words. "She's my wife and won't get away that easy. I have my ways of finding things out."

PLEASE, be ever vigilant. I worry about you daily and know that Charles does as well, even though he does not speak of it. I see him staring at your picture sometimes with great sadness.

Also, PLEASE write more often so that I know you are well. We miss you more than words can say.

Your loving sister,
Mary

- THIRTY-SEVEN -

News From Town

LUNENBURG COUNTY, NOVA SCOTIA - JULY, 1918

Since Andrew's departure, Emma's existence centered around the arrival of letters and her growing certitude that she was indeed carrying his baby. She leaned her head against the warm body of the cow she was milking and pondered her situation. At this time, it would be unfair to share her pregnancy news with Mary who would want to come to her, even though she was in too delicate a condition for travel. After three miscarriages, Mary could not be placed at risk. She would not survive the loss of another babe. Emma was also saddened by the impossibility of assisting Mary when her birthing time came. She would have to let her know.

It was also unfair to burden Andrew with the worry of the childbirth. She would let him know when the child arrived safely.

Then there was Louisa. She felt a growing kinship with this kind, hard-working woman who shared the heartache of Andrew's absence. She must be told. Louisa would be pleased to have a grandchild and would be able to help her when the time came, that being, to the best of her reckoning, in early October, a month after Mary's birthing date.

Also, she was troubled by the yearning looks from Robert, coupled with an anger simmering beneath the surface. Louisa had told her that the brothers had been rivals since they were young boys. Robert was always jealous of his older brother who was bigger and stronger. He had left for the army to prove his worth, but now, with the loss of his arm, the feeling of envy was sharp as a blade. Emma kept him at a distance. Perhaps the news of her pregnancy would make her untouchable.

The sound of a wagon straightened her back. The dogs, dozing by her side lifted their heads and jumped to their feet to bark a welcome. It was Robert returning from town. He had taken to spending the night in Lunenburg with friends who had also returned wounded from the war, but he did not share their stories with the women. In this he showed them kindness. She hurried to finish the milking. There would be letters.

She ran to Robert as he was unhitching the wagon. He silently reached into his pocket and handed her a letter, watching as she tore at the envelope.

France
June 5, 1918

Dearest Emma

Thank you for your parcel that arrived last month. The preserves and baked goods awakened loving memories of you and home.

So much has happened since my last letter and the hurried training in Halifax. My experience during hunting season has been an asset. Although initially I had some difficulty substituting a human for a deer in the sights of my rifle, this all changed when comrades fell at my side - the ultimate reminder that Germany must be held back.

Up to now I have participated in only minor skirmishes, but that will soon change. I have now joined the fourth division that has been involved in major battles. When Commander Watson learned of my fluency in German he assigned me to night reconnaissance duty. We are on the vital edge of victory and my contribution can be valuable. I will fear not, since I know your prayers are with me.

There may be little time to write in the next few weeks Keep well, my love, and know that my thoughts are always with you.

Your devoted,
Andrew

Robert watched as Emma read her letter, watched as her face slowly faded from sunshine to the deepest shades of gloom. He had to ask. "What is the news?"

"Andrew has been assigned to night reconnaissance duty. He is now in the fourth division in France." She sat down suddenly, eyes dark. "I am so afraid for him."

Hans and Helga, who had become her shadows, came to her side nudging her gently. They watched her with droopy eyes, whining, licking her hand. She stooped to bury her face in their fur and receive their kisses. They always sensed her sadness.

Robert frowned and tried to think of words to console her. One thing was sure. This was not the time to tell her he had seen a person in the Lunenburg tavern asking questions about her who fit the description of Edgar.

He had heard Emma's stories of her husband and did not like the look of the man or the manner in which he spoke of her. As he showed her photograph around the bar, the twisted mouth and shifty looks that scanned the faces of his friends had filled Robert with dread. With muscles like rawhide tanned by salt and sun and deep furrows surrounding his ever-moving eyes, Edgar loomed large and menacing.

"Any of ya ruffians seen this woman? I wouldn't put it past her ta be seen with the likes of ya. But she's my wife and needs ta be back where she belongs."

Andrew had been right to remove Emma from his clutches. He held no respect for women. It was frightening to imagine what she had endured.

In the days that followed Robert kept a loaded gun at the ready, both in the house and in the barn. When time allowed, he practiced shooting. The revelation of her pregnancy inspired him even more to the role of protector, not for his brother's sake, but because she was the precious jewel he longed to possess.

- THIRTY-EIGHT -

Edgar's Return

LUNENBURG COUNTY, NOVA SCOTIA - AUGUST 15, 1918

As he was returning the leashed dogs to the barn, Robert heard Emma's scream followed by German curses that could only be the familiar anger of his Mother. The two shepherds, straining on the ropes, began barking madly, their ears twitching. From across the field Robert saw a man dragging Emma's limp form along the coastal path towards an automobile. His mother sat on the ground outside the house clutching at her hip and shouting venom at the fleeing man. The dogs' bodies pulled harder, quivering with anxiety, ready to spring like arrows from a bow. Letting go of their leashes, Robert gave the command to attack. With long strides, he sprinted to the barn for his rifle.

In lightening time, the shepherds were on the swarthy man, snapping at his throat and biting at his legs. Forced to let go of Emma, he tried to beat them off with his arms.

"Git off me ya fuckin' devils." He spun in circles sputtering oaths.

Avoiding his blows, the larger male managed to get one arm in its lethal jaws. A cracking sound was followed by his shriek as the arm bone snapped. Edgar fell to the ground immobilized by the grip of searing pain, unable to fend off the young bitch that now tore at his jugular, silencing him forever.

Robert arrived in time to watch Edgar's death throes, as crimson rivulets spurted from his throat. The growling dogs were still pulling at the body. He called in soothing tones, "Hans, Helga, come." Grabbing their leashes once more, he approached Emma's still body. The dogs whimpered and began licking her face until Robert pushed them aside to lift her head off the cold ground.

Eyes fluttered open. She tried to rise and look around but fell back. Her bulging belly throbbed with the exertion and her hand moved towards the pain.

Robert held her firmly. "Rest easy. All is well."

"What happened? Is Louisa all right?" Her eyes focused on the panting dogs that circled her. "What's wrong with the dogs? What is that red on them?" she stammered. A coppery smell filled her nostrils. Then, her vision filled with the horror of Edgar's bloodied body lying motionless near the edge of the precipice. Her voice was barely audible over the pounding surf below.

"Oh, dear God! Is he dead?"

Robert eased her down and walked over to the body, now surrounded by a patch of blood-soaked earth. "This piece of garbage will never bother you again." With his one good arm, he rolled the lifeless form roughly over the edge and watched it fall into the churning waters below.

Despite her sore hip, Louisa fussed over Emma like a mother hen. She made her a relaxing herbal tea and insisted she eat some soup. Not only was the girl precious to her, but she was carrying a precious first grandchild. The shock of the day's events had been hard on Emma. Louisa watched with satisfaction as the herbal tea took effect.

"A little rest will bring her back. She is strong," Louisa muttered to herself. "Robert and I will make sure nothing else harms her."

Although she did not entirely approve of Robert's disposal of Edgar, she could see his reasoning. An investigation at the farm would be stressful and bring disgrace to Emma at this delicate time. If Edgar's body was found, that being unlikely with the tides as high as they were right now, it would be deemed an accident that happened farther up the coast. Robert had the foresight to move the automobile when he found the keys on the ground.

"God works in mysterious ways," Louisa clucked to herself as she pulled the comforter up to Emma's sleeping face.

- THIRTY-NINE -

Not Worthy

MAHONE BAY, NOVA SCOTIA - DECEMBER, 1985

All week Laura immersed herself in Emma's story, but tonight she had to take a break. She tossed and turned in her bed unable to get the visualization of Edgar's death out of her brain. There was no reason to pity him. Robert and the dogs were Emma's friends and they set her free. Yet her fear of dogs made the bloody scene more horrific in her mind. The scars remained from the bites she received as a child when the neighbor's guard dog broke its leash and viciously attacked her. The two events merged in her consciousness spiking a fear and unease she could not dispel. Yet it was more than that.

The clock struck midnight before the web of sleep finally descended enveloping her in a calming scent of lavender. Outside her door a familiar hollow voice echoed eerily in the hallway.

Laura, he was not worthy...not worthy...not worthy.

Then, a nightmare vision of Emma appeared to her in a flash - her face glowing with unearthly light, her eyes darting flames through the blowing snow. She is standing in the middle of a road wearing a flowing white robe, arms stretched forward with fingers pointing, black hair twisting like hissing snakes around her head. Her lips snarl a silent sentence, over and over like a curse. Headlights appear over the hill, moving rapidly towards her. Then, suddenly, brake lights glow red as blood. The car skids in manic turns. High-pitched screams of terror shatter the dark night as the swerving, spinning vehicle leaps into a deep, dark void.

Laura bolted up, starkly awake and trembling. This was not the Emma of her writing. Every fiber in her body told her that this Emma was possessed by a consuming anger.

What kept Laura sleepless long into the night was the question "Why?"

The next morning, unrested and bleary-eyed, she clutched a cup of coffee with shaking hands. She sat at her desk to continue writing, but her head was still spinning with the night's horrendous vision. This nightmare was not related to Emma's history or her love of Andrew as the other visitations had been. It made no sense.

Her troubled thoughts were interrupted by a knock at the door. She rose to answer with a sense of unease. It didn't sound like Rosie's gentle tapping. She was startled to see a tall uniformed RCMP officer at the door.

"Mrs. McGinty?"

"Yes, can I help you?"

"I'd like to come in if I may. I have some news about your husband."

Laura showed him into the living room, her stomach churning with an acid premonition.

He turned towards her with furrowed brow and sagging lines around a mouth struggling to find the words.

Her voice quavered sounding strange in her ears. "What is it?"

"I'm afraid I've some bad news. We've found what appears to be your husband's body in his car in a gully at the side of highway 103. It looks as if it skidded off the road and was there for at least a week, possibly buried during that last snow storm. I'm sorry Mrs. McGinty."

As he reached to grab her, a sense of unreality spun her down into a chair. The terrifying vision slammed her in the face once more. Could it actually have happened because of Emma? Last night's words from the hallway echoed in her head.

He was not worthy...not worthy...not worthy.

- FORTY -

A Time For Funerals

MAHONE BAY, NOVA SCOTIA – DECEMBER 1985

Laura walked unsteadily through the next few days as if taking part in a bizarre movie of someone else's life. Ray did offer to stay with her as soon as she called with the news, but with so many emotions churning, she needed time to think things through. She tried to let him down gently by telling him that she needed to stay with Rosie through the holidays. It was a strange Christmas, but they made the best of it, considering the circumstances. Instead of planning a festive dinner, they planned a funeral.

Thank God for Rosie's support when she went to identify the body. Her nightmare surfaced again. Although Ted's eyes were closed, his face was contorted unnaturally. There was no doubt that he had seen Emma's flashing eyes searing through the darkness. She clung to her old friend as if grasping for something, someone, she could understand.

Later, when they were sitting around the kitchen table drinking coffee spiked with rum, Rosie took Laura's hand and said in her best maternal voice, "Ya've not said a word all the way home. I know there's something yer not tellin' me that's causin' ya grief. Ya know ya can tell Rosie anythin' without judgement. So, let loose of it, girl."

Laura had not wanted to upset her with the haunting vision, but knew Rosie would not relent. So, like flood waters over a dam, her fears came tumbling out. "It was Emma that caused Ted's death, a totally different kind of Emma than I had ever seen before. I saw her in a dream the night before the police came. I could see it clearly. She came at him in the middle of the highway looking like a demon, chanting curses, threatening him, causing him to go off the road. It scared the hell out of me."

Rosie sat straight back in the chair, with wide blinking eyes. "Well, I never! I guess there was a reason for Emma ta start hauntin' the house after all. There's always a reason. From what I read in the journal, she had no likin' for cruel men so I can see how Ted might of pissed her off."

Noticing the paleness of Laura's face, she patted her hand. "Don't fret, now. I don't think she'll harm you...of all people." Then her face turned fiery and her long braid bounced behind a head bobbing in agitation. "Besides, she'd have ta deal with me in the hereafter if she ever hurt you."

Laura tried not to laugh at the fierce face and ruffled feathers displayed by her friend. "She'd be afraid of that for sure, Rosie. I hope you're right, but I'm going to have you on speed dial just in case I have another vision like that one."

The experience of seeing Ted's body had been so numbing that she nearly forgot about her appointment with the gynecologist. Ray didn't. She returned home to find he had called and said he would pick her up the next day.

Right on time, he insisted on going into the office with her and held her hand throughout. A wave of relief washed over them with the news that the tumor was benign. At least one thing in her life was returning to normal. It was tempting to stay with Ray for a night, but she needed to do some emotional house cleaning before she could feel at ease in his company again.

The hurdles that remained were the funeral and the phone calls to Ted's two younger brothers. Their mother had left them when he was a teenager, and their father drank himself to death shortly after. The boys never got along and did not keep in touch. Abrasive personalities, as well as drinking, ran in the family. She was sure they would not travel half way across the country to attend. Aunt Rosie and Reverend Darcy would help her with the details. It would be a simple affair with possibly only a few of his co-workers attending. For them, she would have to wear the widow's mask of sorrow. In her heart, and with only a slight sense of guilt, she began to feel the joy of liberation.

When she was finally alone in the house the night of the funeral, her imagination took flight. Her reality merged with Emma's past in bizarre thoughts leading to unsettling questions. Was Emma her avenging angel guiding her along a new path? Could she see into Laura's heart? Or was she an evil spirit that would always haunt her grandmother's house? As if in answer to her thoughts the lavender scent filled the room and the hollow voice echoed in the hallway once more. This time the tone was gentle.

"He was unworthy. Finish now, and the debt will be paid... will be paid...will be paid."

She went to her typewriter. The message was clear. Emma's tale needed to be completed to give them both peace. Immersion in the sad ending could no longer be avoided.

In Emma's story, it was also a time of funerals.

- FORTY-ONE -

Robert's Departure

LUNENBURG COUNTY, NOVA SCOTIA - SEPTEMBER, 1918

As she sat on the porch shelling peas, Emma periodically searched the road for Robert's wagon. He would return soon from his weekly trip into Lunenburg. Weeks had passed since Andrew's last letter and she awaited the post with growing concern. Although encouraged by newspaper reports of allied victories, she knew Andrew was in the thick of the conflict.

The strong inside kick to her ribs made her flinch, reminding her that the birth of their child was imminent. Now that Edgar was gone, it was a relief to be able to tell Mary of her whereabouts and her pregnancy. Mary was in recovery after the birth of their son, Charles, and hopefully would be strong enough to assist when Emma's time came. Against Louisa's advice, she had also told Mary about Edgar's death. It seemed sinful to be so happy about her freedom from him, but even the pious Mary said that she was glad and that he deserved such an end. Emma released Mary from her promise not to tell Charles of her whereabouts. She was sure he would bring Mary as soon as she sent word that the baby was coming.

A cloud of dust caught her attention. It was not like Robert to drive the horses so. When the wagon pulled up to the house, she rose in alarm to see him pale and slumped over in pain.

"Please, Emma…help me down."

His shirt, covered in vomit, had a vile smell, and was tinged with red.

"Oh, Robert, you poor man. What has happened?"

"It's the flu I fear. It has taken me suddenly. I felt so weak I could barely make it home."

She took the large man by his good arm as he slowly climbed down from the wagon, at the same time shouting as loudly as she could, "Louisa, come help. Robert is ill."

Louisa poked her head from around the barn door and saw the struggling pair. Sprinting like a young girl, with the dogs in eager pursuit, she was soon at Robert's side making clucking sounds about Emma not exerting herself too much. The two women soon had Robert in the house. As soon as Louisa assessed his condition, she banned Emma from his room, no longer allowing her to touch him nor any of his things. Their faces lined with worry as his fever rose, and he fell into a fretful sleep.

Reports of the deadly Spanish flu had been in the newspapers. Throughout the community schools were being closed and public gatherings restricted. There seemed to be little that could be done for the afflicted except prayers and burials. Only the very strong survived.

Emma paced the living room restlessly as she waited for Louisa to come out of Robert's bedroom. She stopped to comfort the dogs who also waited with their muzzles on their paws, eyes drooping.

When the door opened, Louisa's ashen face told all. Emma approached to embrace her but Louisa raised a prohibiting hand. "No, you must not come near me or Robert for the baby's sake. I will manage. But there was a letter in his pocket. If you will permit me I will do my best to read it to you."

Although her heart ached for Louisa, they both wanted to know what the letter contained. "Yes, please read it. Let us hope for good news on this of all days."

Louise read on haltingly, uncertain of some of the words, stopping to smile at Emma when he spoke of love.

France
August 20, 1918

Dearest Emma,

I write hoping that you have heard of the allied victory at Amiens. I could not describe the horrors of the conflict without falling into the deepest sorrow. Perhaps, when I am home holding you in my arms it will be possible. I am confident we will put the Germans in their place, and it will be over soon.

We have captured many prisoners, so I have been assigned to the interrogation of officers. I cannot tell you more, but it is an unpleasant business. Worse yet, many are ill. It is pitiful to see such agonies with little we can do for them.

Your letters are the only sunshine of my days and color the dreams of my nights. They give me hope of a future full of happiness when I am reunited with the one holding the key to all that I desire. Please keep writing even though I cannot reply often.

Be well my love.

Your devoted,
Andrew

Emma searched Louisa's face when she finished reading and tried to read her thoughts. The startled eyes, twitching with anxiety told her she was experiencing the same dread.

What was this illness he spoke of? Surely not the one that they were now witnessing!

Robert appeared worse the next morning. As she waited for the doctor, Louisa bathed his brow with cold cloths in an attempt to quell the ferocious fever. In his delirious state, she was unable to give him water and watched helplessly as his skin turned a pale blue and his breathing became labored. She lifted him up to help him breath. But as his lungs continued to fill with fluid, he gasped for breath, choked as if drowning, then splattered the bed covers with a spray of crimson.

Louisa let out an agonized cry. "Dear God in heaven save him! He cannot leave us now!"

Emma ran to the bedroom door to watch the weeping woman holding Robert's bloodied face to her bosom, her prayers unheeded. With his sudden death, a cold wave of grief and fear washed over the two women, leaving them frozen in a sea of pain.

- FORTY-TWO -

Katrina's Birth

LUNENBURG COUNTY, NOVA SCOTIA - SEPTEMBER, 1918

A week of mourning etched rivers on Louisa's face. The doctor had arranged for help with the burial but a proper funeral was not possible since gatherings had been banned for public safety. The two women read from the Bible at the family gravesite on the crest of a hill overlooking the sea. It was a peaceful place with the sound of waves echoing off the cliff.

Emma worried about Louisa's lack of appetite, her current frailty. They continued the work on the farm, tending to the animals, relying on kind neighbors to assist with the harvest. But Louisa often lost her train of thought and had to be reminded of the tasks that needed to be done next. By evening they were both exhausted.

Tonight was particularly bad. All day Emma was feeling uncomfortable with the weight of the baby. She realized the pains she had been feeling in her abdomen might be the onset of labor. Rising from her bed, a sudden contraction doubled her over, and she felt a rush of liquid flow down her legs.

With a gasp, she called out loudly "Louisa, please come. It is time."

Immediately, the woman appeared at her side wearing a nightgown. Her face flushed with excitement accentuating the deep folds lining her brow, she took Emma's wrist feeling her pulse. "How often are the pains coming, my child?"

"About every five minutes I think." But suddenly another spasm came with frightening sharpness. She laid back trying to hold in her agony, arms folded over her belly. When it passed, she cried out, "Louisa, please get word to Mary."

Taking Emma's hand. She smiled and spoke quickly in a soothing voice. "Don't worry, my dear. Try to stay calm. It will take some time yet, but I can help you. I have assisted many midwifes in my day. But if you wish it, I will get the neighbor's boy to go for Mary."

"Yes, please Louisa! I think something is wrong."

No longer smiling, Louisa placed her hands over Emma's bulging belly, then placed her ear down to listen for the fetal heartbeat, first below her navel and then above it. She looked away from Emma to hide the worry. "Yes, I'll go now and will be back soon." Throwing on a robe, Louisa scurried towards the door calling instructions over her shoulder. "Breathe deeply when the pains come, and try to rest when they stop, just like I showed you. We will bring this baby into the world soon."

By the time Louisa returned Emma's contractions had become stronger and closer together. Her cries pierced the heart of the older woman. She feared Emma was right. The baby was large and in a breech position. The only breech delivery she had watched had ended badly. She went to the kitchen to find her sharpest knife, the one she used to butcher the lamb...and slipped it into the pocket of her robe. Then, fighting the weariness in her bones, Louisa brought cold cloths to wipe Emma's fevered forehead and rubbed her back between contractions, all the while softly chanting prayers for these two precious lives. As dawn was breaking, she scanned the window often, wringing her hands, searching the road.

Where is Mary? She should be here by now!

A cry rang out like the howl of an injured animal. "Louisa! It's coming!"

The anguish in the sound shattered her thoughts, and she flinched as Emma's tense arm reached out to squeeze her gnarled arthritic fingers. More tortured sounds escaped from Emma's core. Her face and hair were drenched with sweat as she struggled with the next contraction.

In the short interval between the spasms of pain she whispered hoarsely, "Louisa, promise me you will save my baby no matter what. It may be all that survives of the love Andrew and I have." Her voice rose shrilly with the pain. "Promise! Please Louisa!"

Louisa's weathered face softened, her eyes glistening,

as she beheld the pleading woman who was so young, so important to her son. "Hush child. Save your strength. I promise I will do all I can to save Andrew's child." Her heart vibrating with determination, she uncovered Emma's outstretched knees to see the round pink bottom of her little cherub struggling to enter the world.

The dogs barked franticly from the barn as Mary pounded on the door. "Emma, Louisa, are you there?" No response. She tried a few more times then turned the handle and entered the silent greyness of the sitting room. At first, when she saw the old woman rocking the babe in her arms she was filled with joy. Then she saw the crimson footsteps from the bedroom...the woman's bloodied robe.

"Where's Emma?"

Clutching the babe tightly to her, Louisa turned towards Mary with drooping eyelids and a face drained of tears. She pointed towards the bedroom door and faintly whispered, "I did what I promised. I could not save her too. God have mercy on my soul."

In a flash, the scene in the bedroom burned into Mary's mind as if it had been branded with fire. On the bed in a halo of dampened curls Emma's pale body lay peacefully in a pool of blood. There was a deep cut in her abdomen. One arm was spread out at her side as if she were holding her child. A knife lay on the floor next to Louisa's footsteps.

Mary ran to the bed and wailed as she fell to her

knees. "My dear sweet girl, what has she done to you! If only we had gotten here sooner, I might have saved you."

Hearing her cries, Charles rushed into the house carrying their own newborn son. When he entered the bedroom, he came to Mary's side trembling with a rage he had rarely shown before. "Good God in heaven, has it come to this? How can we have lost her now!" Lifting Mary to him with his free arm, he tried to grapple with the grief he had seen too often in the faces of others. Only now did he truly understand the depths of sorrow a loved one's loss could bring.

After placing the babe in a cradle, Louisa came to the door and spoke softly to Charles in broken sentences. "You are a man of God. Believe me... I swear to you... on all that is holy. I could not save her. The babe was stuck... a cord around her neck...dying. Emma made me promise... to save her... no matter what." Then, heaving an anguished sigh, she continued with her last strength. "Too much blood...could not stop it. But Emma held her daughter...before she died. I loved her too...almost as much as my sons."

No longer able to stand, she collapsed in a chair, bent shoulders heaving, hands covering her face.

- FORTY-THREE -

Resolutions

MAHONE BAY, NOVA SCOTIA — NOVEMBER, 1918

A week had passed since the funeral. Mary's grieving was mixed with a strong concern about leaving Emma's child with Louisa. The woman was overwhelmed with farm chores now that all help was gone. She seemed weakened by all that had happened, not in her right mind at times. But what could she do about it. Louisa was the child's grandmother. Andrew, the father, would soon return.

Charles would not condone acknowledgement of the child. A child out of wedlock would reflect badly on his sister and on him. He wished to have it kept secret and to let Andrew and his mother be responsible for the child. Charles would not hear of Mary taking the baby. His angry resentment still rang in her ears. "I won't have her! She and those Burgess people have taken Emma from us. I will not have them disgrace our family name as well. As far as anyone outside the family knows, Emma Lindsay Harkness left with her husband Edgar to live in the Caribbean."

He could barely contain his anger during the short funeral service he conducted when the three of them placed Emma in the ground, in the Burgess family plot. They all agreed that the name on the headstone would be Emma Burgess. That is what she would have wanted. Charles ordered a large stone inscribed with an epitaph of his own design but could not bear to visit the site after it was installed.

Mary checked on Louisa and the babe as often as she could, but now, her life was turning upside down with the move. At long last, Charles was recognized for his abilities; he was being posted to Halifax as an administrative assistant to the bishop, a position he had been seeking for some time. In a few short weeks, the rectory would be sold since the new one was now completed. Maurice and Suzette Dauphinee, the new prospective owners, arrive tomorrow to inspect the place. She must make the house look tidy and well cared for. What with baby Charles still keeping her up most of the night, she could barely find the energy to get through the day and certainly had no strength left to stand against the iron will of her husband.

However, she continued her visitations with Katrina until the day before they left for Halifax. A hope remained in her heart that they would keep her in the family, one way or another.

One month later, as she was still in the process of unpacking their belongings in Halifax, Mary received a letter addressed to her from the Dauphinees.

Mahone Bay, N.S.
December 1, 1918

Dear Mrs. Lindsay,

We received a visitor yesterday looking for you, an elderly farmer from Lunenburg County. He informed us of the death of Louisa Burgess who apparently had heart failure last Friday. They had been keeping an eye on her of late due to her poor health and were alarmed when they saw the soldier come to her farm that morning. His wife went over after chores, and their fears were confirmed. Louisa's son, Andrew, had died in France of the same Spanish flu that took her other son. She found Louisa collapsed on the floor, clutching the delivered letter. She was unable to revive her.

They have been looking after the baby, which she named Katrina, but can no longer do so. Since you knew the baby's mother, they wondered whether you would know of any relatives who could take her. We advised him that we would get in touch with you and let him know as soon as possible. In the meantime, we suggested we could care for the child which they accepted gratefully.

We realize you do not know us very well, but we are

honest, God-fearing people who are financially secure. We have been trying to have a child for many years now and are hoping that this might be the answer to our prayers. If you do not know of any relatives of Katrina, we would very much like to adopt her. We could provide you with references to assure you that we would raise her in a safe and loving home.

Please let us know your answer as soon as possible since we are already growing fond of the child. If the adoption can take place, perhaps your husband could advise us of the best way to proceed. We will be looking daily for your reply.

Yours sincerely,
Maurice and Suzette Dauphinee

After reading the letter, Mary sat down to ponder all that had happened in the past year with a torrent of emotions – sadness for poor Louisa and the loss of her family; happiness that Katrina could have a good home with the Dauphinees; and a hope that Charles would agree to take the baby now. She went to his study and knocked on the door.

"Charles, I have some disturbing news." She handed him the letter and sat down to watch his face as he read. His heavy eyebrows drew together tightly, then released. There was sadness in his eyes, but also relief, until he viewed her hope-filled face.

"Mary, you cannot be thinking of taking the child. It

would not be right. Do you not see that God has placed Katrina into the hands of people who will love her without question and will maintain secrecy about her parentage? I can make arrangements for her adoption as a child of deceased parents. She would be registered as Katrina Dauphinee. I am sure the Dauphinees will agree to secrecy in the matter, if I assure them it is the only way the adoption will go through unchallenged."

Tears began to form in the corners of Mary's eyes. "But, Charles, she is all we have left of Emma."

"I know." He sighed. "I no longer feel anger towards the babe or the Burgess family. How can I with the tragedy of their lost lives. But I feel it would be best for Katrina not to be labelled a bastard. Secrecy is key."

Mary stood up and quickly wiped the streaks from her face. "Perhaps you are right. I'll send a letter to the Dauphinees today to let them know that if they will agree to secrecy, you will make arrangements."

He rose to kiss her cheek tenderly. "Thank you." By way of appeasement he added, "I'd have no objection, if you wish to still visit the child, Mary."

As she walked to the privacy of her bedroom Mary accepted the wisdom of his unspoken words. The adoption would also protect Charles from any scandal.

Sitting at her roll-top desk, she quickly scribed a response to the Dauphinees, inserting an additional request to be Katrina's godparent, then took out her journal and vowed that someday, Emma's story would be told.

- FORTY-FOUR -

COMPLETION

MAHONE BAY AND HALIFAX, NOVA SCOTIA - JANUARY, 1986

The narrative was finished at last. Laura felt drained physically and emotionally. So much heartache through those difficult times! Under the circumstances, how fortunate for the family that the Dauphinees had taken in baby Katrina, her grandmother. Yet, it was the love that Emma had for Andrew and her baby that affected Laura most. That Emma had extracted a promise from Louisa to save the baby, no matter what, was her ultimate sacrifice to preserve a part of Andrew's love. In a sense, baby Katrina was a genetic gift Emma had passed on to following generations. Knowing about the love story of Katrina's true parents somehow explained why there had been such a strong bond between Laura, her mother, and her grandmother. On her desk, the last photo they had taken together reminded her of all the happy times. She pulled out two more photos. After studying them carefully, she made a promise to honor her ancestors in her own special way.

There was also another promise that was weighing on her mind. She had made an extra copy of her manuscript for Rosie to read. She had given her the journal some time ago, but the version she had created with Emma had so much more to add. Rosie had been very patient in a Rosie kind of way, only calling once a day.

"Have ya finished yet, Laura? Ya knows I'm old and could kick the bucket any day. If I meets Emma on her turf, I wants ta be able ta discuss it with her ta see if ya got it right."

Now she could let Rosie know it was finally done. Preparing to venture out into the cold to drop it off, she decided to ask Rosie if she could borrow Bugsy once more. There could be no waiting until his weekend visit. She must give Ray the final pages now. After all, it was the beginning of a new year, and she felt like celebrating her accomplishment.

When she got to Ray's house he opened the door immediately, welcoming her with hugs and a bottle of wine. "It's time for some relaxation. You've been through a lot lately and working much too hard at this."

"I couldn't agree more, but read first. I need to know your thoughts about the ending. I will drink wine," Laura said, as she took the bottle from his hands.

Ray put down the last page and flashed his magnetic smile. "Laura that's an amazing story. You've done a great job. I just happen to know a local publisher who will want to see this."

"Thanks Ray. Right now, I'm exhausted. Getting to know Emma has been a very emotional time for me. Mary's writing made the difference. She was a loyal friend throughout. I feel a real kinship to her, and without her written words I would never have known about my true ancestry. I may even have cousins I don't know about through Mary's son, Charles. Rosie often visited her in the nursing home years ago. She would remember if Charles had any children."

"Finding lost relatives sounds like your next project." Ray grasped both her hands and looked into her eyes. "Do you know that you've discovered why you're such a special person?"

Laura beamed back at him. "No. Why?"

"Because you are Emma and Andrew's sole descendent, in effect a living remembrance of their love. She died so that their baby could live. That's why she's so protective of you. She's depending on you to pass on their genes."

Laura's face awakened as if bright lights flooded her darkened room. "Oh my God, Ray. I never saw it that way. It makes sense now. She hated Ted. That's why he wasn't worthy to be part of her continuing family."

"Well I sure hope she likes me. I plan to stick around."

"You would know by now, if she didn't."

"In fact," he said with a twinkle of his azure eyes, "fatherhood is something I might have in mind for the future."

Laura returned his gaze with a mischievous grin. "In fact", she mimicked, "I'm sure I heard her say something about it being time for another descendent and… she likes blue eyes."

He scooped her into a bear hug and whispered in her ear, "Princess, our bedroom awaits."

Epilogue

MAHONE BAY, N.S. – JULY, 1992

… six years later

Instead of feeling the grief of the past, Laura now embraced the memories of her family and this house that she transformed into her home. She contemplated the accomplishment with pride. The work was now completed. The refinished oak woodwork shone throughout, contrasting darkly against the newly painted walls; its distinctive grain prominent once more. The three upstairs bedrooms had all been repainted in pastel shades of lavender, pink and blue with matching brocade curtains.

There was a corner of the attic that was her very own, set up as an office. She could continue her writing there without distractions, taking an occasional break up on the widow's walk to breathe in the fresh salt air, gaze upon the dancing waters, and enjoy the serenity of her beloved town.

On the first floor, the living room's sculpted ceiling glistened with hints of gold accentuating its ornate patterns; the fireplace with its refurbished mantle and brass fittings added to the cozy charm of the room. The kitchen was modernized with new appliances complementing Kate's wood stove. Laura was pleased with the embroidered wall hangings, lace curtains, and old pottery she had found at the Sunday flea market. They enhanced the Victorian décor perfectly.

Her best finds, however, were the carved, antique frames for the portraits she had painted of her family. One painting was from the photo on her desk of herself, her mother and her grandparents; the second was from the wedding picture of her parents; the other two were from the photos of Emma and Andrew, taken from Mary's journal. They all hung prominently by the dining room table.

The ancestors would be pleased.

As she moved towards the garden door she rubbed her belly to ease the little kicks she had been feeling all day. "I think this one will be a soccer player," she thought. Even though she knew she would have to go through another caesarian delivery, she couldn't wait. He would be born in the best facilities in Halifax with her trusted doctor. Doc MacKinnon was the best.

She heard the car door slam and peered out through the old-fashioned screen door. "Emma May, where are you? Daddy just got home and supper will be ready soon."

"I'm playing with the nice lady, Mommy."

Holding onto her bulging belly, Laura made her way, as briskly as she could, through the flowering rose arbor leading to the garden. She found her daughter surrounded by tiger lilies and Shasta daisies sitting in her sand box. She smiled up at her with dimpled cheeks and eyes bluer than the sky.

Catching her breath and trying not to sound alarmed Laura asked, "What nice lady, Emma May?"

"I like her. She has fun stories. We are making our own garden around the castle."

Laura brushed the dark curls from the child's forehead, "I don't see anyone, dear. Is she your secret friend?"

"No, silly. That's Jojo. This is a grownup. She's pretty and smiles a lot. She has a beautiful sparkle dress. She said she used to live in our house and guess what."

"What, honey."

"Her name is Emma too!"

In a maternal panic, Laura's heart skipped a beat. She clutched the child to her. She had not seen Emma's ghost since she had finished her story.

Should she be concerned for her daughter? Were the haunting nights going to continue?

As she was about to rise with Emma May and run to the house, Laura became aware of a tugging at her shirt.

"Mommy, wait. My friend Emma says don't worry. She's very happy now. She says you are most worthy. What does worthy mean?"

Laura sat back down and hugged the child sitting her on the ground beside her. She sighed with relief and thought back to the day she found Emma's grave site. It was on the old Burgess property that was now occupied by a young couple. The family plot was surrounded by a riot of pink and purple lupines, fenced off on a hill overlooking the bluff. It contained graves dating back to the early nineteenth century. Emma's was the largest headstone, next to the one for Andrew. They were surrounded by a cluster of forget-me-nots and a patch of fragrant lavender. The thought of her epitaph still made her shiver.

May the future children for whom she died prove worthy of such a sacrifice.

Emma May's insistent voice brought her back to the present. "Mommy! Do you know what it means?"

Laura struggled to find a way of explaining to a five-year-old. "Yes, dear. It's an old-fashioned word. It means someone is pleased with you, like when they give you a gift and you do something special with it that makes them happy."

"Did she give you a gift, Mommy?"

"Yes, she did. She gave it a long time ago - to me, to you, and to your baby brother. When you are older and understand about being a woman, I will tell you all about our Emma and her gift."

About The Author

Kat Karpenko has had a varied writing career in technical writing, journalism, and short stories. This is her first novel which originally started as a short story. Born in Windsor, Ontario, Canada, she has also lived in England and Australia, but has spent most of her life in Nova Scotia where she worked in various administrative capacities at Dalhousie University in Halifax. Now retired, she divides her time between Mazatlán, Mexico and Canada.

katkarpenkoauthor.wordpress.com
authorkkarpenko@gmail.com
facebook.com/authorkatkarpenko

Made in the USA
San Bernardino, CA
08 March 2017